Witch Is When The Hammer Fell

Published by Implode Publishing Ltd
© Implode Publishing Ltd 2016

The right of Adele Abbott to be identified as the Author of the Work has been asserted by her in accordance with the Copyright, Designs and Patents Act 1988.

All rights reserved, worldwide.
No part of this publication may be reproduced, stored in a retrieval system, or transmitted, in any form or by any means without the prior written permission of the copyright owner.

The characters and events in this book are fictitious. Any similarity to real persons, dead or alive, is purely coincidental and not intended by the author.

Chapter 1

I was still half asleep when I stepped out of my flat, and bumped into Luther Stone.

"Oh hi, Jill," he said in that sexy voice of his. "I was hoping I might see you."

"Morning, Luther."

Hoping to see me, eh? That sounded promising. I hadn't seen his sidekick, Lucinda, for a while. Maybe he'd seen the error of his ways, and dumped her. Perhaps he'd realised there was someone much closer to home who was just right for him.

"There's something I'd like to show you," he said. "When you have a moment."

"What's that?" My curiosity was piqued.

"That would be telling. It's a surprise."

Normally, I hated surprises. But a surprise from Luther Stone? That was different.

"Are you free tomorrow, after work?"

"Tomorrow? Let me think." Yes! Yes! Yes! "I think that should be okay. What time did you have in mind?"

"How about six o'clock? Could you come to my flat then?"

"I'll do my best." Just try stopping me!

As soon as I was in the car, I called Kathy. I had to let her know the latest development.

"Jill? Do you realise what time it is? I'm trying to get the kids ready for school. Is something wrong?"

"I have important news."

"Do you mean *real* important news, or *your kind* of important news?"

"Luther Stone—"

"Oh, *that* kind of important news."

"No listen, Kathy. This time there's no mistake. He wants me to go around to his flat tomorrow after work."

"What for?"

"He said it's a surprise."

"Oh dear."

"What do you mean 'oh dear'? It's obviously a good thing. Why else would he ask me to go around there? Maybe he's bought me a present?"

"Why would Luther Stone buy you a present? He's your accountant. Have you forgotten what happened last time you got carried away like this?"

"That was *completely* different. That was just a misunderstanding. How could I have known he just wanted to look at my books? I just got a little carried away."

"A *little* carried away? You bought a new dress, hired a chef and almost set the place on fire with a thousand candles."

"I don't need reminding, thank you. Anyway, as I was trying to tell you, this time he didn't mention my books, or accountancy, or anything like that. He said he had a little surprise for me, and that I should go around to his place at six o'clock tomorrow. Look, I'm too excited to go into work just yet. Can I come over to yours?"

"Right now? It's pandemonium here at the moment."

"I won't get in the way. I promise."

***

When I arrived at Kathy's, Peter was upstairs getting

the kids ready for school.

"So, what do you think?" I said.

"About what?" Kathy was making sandwiches.

"You know what! About Luther Stone and his surprise."

"I think you're getting way ahead of yourself as usual. Why don't you do what normal people do."

"Who wants to be *normal*? Normal is boring."

"I just don't want you to build your hopes up, and end up disappointed again. We don't want a repeat of the last time."

"I wish you'd stop reminding me about that. I told you — that was completely different."

"How was it different?"

"It just was. Anyway, are you going to offer me a cup of tea or what?"

"If you want one, you'll have to make it yourself. I have to get ready for work, and get the kids off to school."

"Okay. Do you want one?"

"Yeah, go on then."

"I thought you might."

I made us both a cup of tea. At least I got the right amount of sugar in mine for a change. The Tupperware box, which should have had my custard creams in it, was empty — as per usual.

"I thought you were going to get some custard creams in for me."

"I will when I have time. Anyway, there are plenty in the tin."

"You know I can't eat those."

"They're perfectly good custard creams. If I'd taken them out of the tin, and put them in your Tupperware box five minutes before you walked in, you'd have been none the wiser."

"Of course I would. I know when a custard cream has been contaminated."

"You need help."

"Anyway." I ignored her remark. "What do you think Luther's surprise might be?"

"I don't know. Maybe he's devised a new accounting system, and he wants to talk you through it?"

"It can't be anything like that. He would have said if it was to do with work. He was being very secretive. The way he spoke—it was very—sexy."

"You're doing it again! You're getting carried away."

"It's definitely not my imagination this time. Maybe he's going to ask me to move in with him?"

"You haven't even been on a date with the man! Of course he isn't going to ask you to move in with him!"

"You don't know that."

"Yes, I do, because I live in the world of the *sane*—unlike you."

"It's no good talking to you. I shouldn't have bothered coming round."

"I did warn you it wasn't a good time."

"I suppose I ought to go then."

"Just a minute. Now you're here, I want to ask you a favour."

"*You* want to ask *me* a favour, after you've spent the last ten minutes criticising me?"

"I haven't been criticising. I've just been trying to make you see sense."

"Says you! What's the favour?"

"It isn't for me, anyway. It's for Lizzie."

"Oh, well, that's different. Does she need me to help her with her homework or something?"

Kathy laughed. "Do you really think I'd ask you to help with her homework? You were hopeless at school."

"I was *not* hopeless!"

"Yes, you were. You always came last in tests."

"You're exaggerating. Anyway, how can I help her?"

"Her teacher has set her class a project. They have to write about the kind of job they'd like to do when they grow up. For some reason, which I can't even begin to understand, Lizzie says she'd like to be a private investigator."

"Did she?" I smirked. "She's obviously seen what an exciting life I lead."

"Yeah—no, it can't be that. Perhaps she's seen one on TV."

"Cheek!"

"Anyway, the teacher said they should spend a day with someone who does the job which they'd like to do. So she wants to spend a day with you to see what it is you do. That's always assuming you do anything at all."

"A day? You mean, like *a whole* day?"

"Yeah, why not? That's what the teacher suggested."

"But what would she do?"

"Go to the office with you, and watch what you do. And then, assuming she doesn't die of boredom, she can write about it when she's back at school."

"But it might be scary for her. I deal with some very dangerous cases."

"Give me a break. You spend most of your time twiddling your thumbs, wondering where your next job is coming from, and talking to your silly cat."

"Winky isn't silly."

"So, can she come with you or not?"

Lizzie ran into the room. "Please, Auntie Jill. Can I? I really want to spend a day at your office because you've got an exciting job. Not like Mummy and Daddy."

"Of course you can, Lizzie. I'd be delighted for you to spend some time with me. But you shouldn't be too hard on your mum and dad—not everyone can have an interesting and exciting job."

Kathy rolled her eyes. "So, can we set a date then?"

"I'll have to check my diary and see what's happening."

"Check your diary?" She laughed. "Is there anything in it?"

"As I was saying—I'll check my diary, to find out when would be the best day, and I'll let you know. Is that okay, Lizzie?"

"Yes. Thanks, Auntie Jill."

Peter told Lizzie to go and clean her teeth.

"Thanks for that," Kathy said. "She'll enjoy a nice, quiet day at your office."

"Well, at least she wants to come to work with me. She doesn't appear to be very interested in spending time at the wool shop with you."

"Just as well. Your grandmother would probably scare her to death. Anyway, there's something else I wanted to ask you."

"Another favour?"

"No. I just thought it would be something you'd enjoy."

If Kathy thinks I'm going to enjoy something, you can be pretty sure I won't.

"What have you got me into this time?"

"I've decided it's about time I got back in shape. I also need a way to relax after work."

"Kathy, what have you signed me up for?"

"It's nothing strenuous."

"Just tell me what it is."

"Yoga."

"I'm not doing yoga."

"Look, it's a free trial. I thought we could both go along, and see what we thought of it."

"*Yoga*? Do you know what they do? You have to stretch your arms and legs into unnatural positions. We could do ourselves a serious injury."

"Stop being such a wimp. You and I are going to yoga. If we don't like it, we needn't go again."

"Do I have a choice?"

"Not really."

"You shouldn't let her push you around." Peter grinned.

"I'll get my own back—don't worry. Anyway, Peter, are you still enjoying working for the colonel?"

"It was the best move I ever made. He's the first employer who's ever shown me any respect. In fact, he doesn't really treat me like an employee at all. More like, I know this sounds stupid, but more like a son. He always asks how the family are. And best of all, he appreciates the work I do. It's just brilliant."

"Does the colonel have any kids? I don't remember him mentioning any."

"Just the one son as far as I'm aware. I get the impression that they aren't very close. From the little he did tell me, it sounds as though his son was on course for a career in engineering. But then as far as I can make out, he dropped out of university and just sort of threw it all away. The colonel glossed over it, but I got the impression that gambling and drink were his son's downfall."

I left Kathy, Peter and the kids to their pandemonium. It gave me a migraine just watching them running around the house, shouting at one another.

***

As I walked up the stairs to the office, I heard a strange noise. It was a sort of buzzing sound. When I pushed open the door, I saw Mrs V in the far corner; she was leaning over a machine of some kind.

"Mrs V!" I shouted.

She couldn't hear me at the best of times, so she had no chance over the sound of that machine; whatever it was.

"Mrs V! What are you doing?"

She still couldn't hear a thing, but then she jumped when she caught sight of me.

"Jill! I didn't hear you come in. Why didn't you say something?"

"I did. I've been shouting at you for the last minute."

"I'm sorry. I couldn't hear you because of the shredder."

"Where did it come from? I didn't order this."

"Those people next door, the Armitages, were throwing it out. Two men were just about to take it downstairs, so I asked them if it worked, and they said it did. They said we could have it if we wanted it. I thought it might come in handy."

"But we don't really have any confidential waste."

"All of our files could be classed as confidential."

"Yes, but we don't need to throw them away."

"But it's such fun. Look." She fed a sheet of paper into the machine.

"It's just a shredder, Mrs V. That's what they do."

"I've never used one before. I didn't realise how exciting they are."

"What's that pile of documents?"

"They're just old files."

"Can I take a look?" I flicked through them. "You can't shred these!"

"Why not, dear? They're just taking up room in the filing cabinet."

"These are recent cases. In fact, a couple of them are still current."

"Are they? I didn't realise."

"You can't just shred any old thing."

"But it makes such pretty confetti."

"I'm sure it does, but the whole idea is that you shred documents which are no longer needed. I think we should get rid of this machine."

"No! Please don't do that," she begged. "Can't we keep it?"

"Okay, but you can't shred anything else without checking with me first. Agreed?"

"Agreed."

Chapter 2

I was at my desk, doing nothing in particular, when I heard the outer door open. There were raised voices, and then the door to my office burst open. It was Grandma.

"Sorry, Jill," Mrs V said. "I tried to stop her."

"It's okay, Mrs V."

"Well, young lady?" Grandma said. "Are you ready?"

Was I meant to be going somewhere with her? Had she told me that I should be ready for something? I searched my memory, but drew a blank.

"Ready for what, Grandma?"

"Ready for your next magic lesson, of course."

"I thought you said that we weren't going to have any more lessons for a while?"

"If you remember, what I actually said was I didn't want you distracted while you were acting as campaign manager for my shot at a seat on the town council. A role in which, I might add, you failed miserably."

"It was a very close result, Grandma."

"Close doesn't cut it, Jill. Am I on the town council?"

"No."

"Did you fail, then?"

"I suppose so."

"That just about sums it up, then. Anyway, now that the campaign's over, there's no reason why your magic lessons can't resume."

"I am rather busy."

"No you're not. Come on, let's get going."

"Right this minute?"

"No time like the present. We're going to the Range."

"Will the twins be there?"

"You won't be having any more lessons with the twins. They're level two, and likely to stay on that level forever. The sooner you work your way up to level six, the better for all concerned."

"I've only been a witch for five minutes!"

"You've been a witch all your life. You may insist you didn't know, but that's no excuse."

"I reached level three in record time."

"What would you like? Some kind of medal?"

"That would be nice."

She gave me a withering look.

"I was only joking."

"Magic is *not* a joking matter. It's very serious. Take my hand and we'll go to the Range now."

"What if Mrs V checks my office? Won't she wonder where we've gone?"

"Annabel is way too focused on her knitting to notice whether you're here or not. Besides, when I came through just now, she was staring at that machine in the corner of the room. I think that old girl is losing her marbles. Come on. Let's get going."

She grabbed my hand with her bony fingers, and the next thing I knew we were at the Range. It had been a while since I'd been there, and it was much quieter than on any of my previous visits. Almost eerily quiet.

"There aren't many people here today, Grandma."

"That's because it's an 'advanced' day."

"What's that?"

"It means that no one below level three is allowed in. That gives the more advanced witches more freedom and space to practise their spells without having to worry about all the amateurs getting in the way."

"Amateurs? That's a bit unfair on the twins, isn't it?"

"I would have thought the twins personified the word 'amateurs'. Anyway, come on. I want to show you something."

"What's going on over there?" I pointed to the far side of the Range.

"Where?" She sounded impatient.

"Over there. It looks like they're playing sports."

"Some witches use sporting activities to practise certain spells. It stops them getting bored. It's mainly things like the 'power' spell, the 'faster' spell and other spells which involve physical exertion. See that young witch over there?"

"The one with the javelin?"

"Yes. Just watch her throw it."

I did. She launched it with such power that it flew the entire length of the Range, landing at the very far side. If she'd been competing in human games, she would have beaten any world record. Then I spotted another young witch.

"What's she doing with that ball and chain?"

"Don't you know anything? It's not a ball and chain. It's called a hammer."

"It doesn't look much like a hammer. What do you do with it?"

"Watch. You'll see."

The young witch began to spin around and around in circles, faster and faster. Then suddenly, she seemed to lose her footing, and the hammer, instead of flying off parallel to the ground, flew up into the air.

"Where's it gone?" I watched it disappear through the clouds.

"Probably into the stratosphere somewhere. Come on, we don't have all day to hang around here. Let's get going."

She led me to another part of the Range I hadn't seen before. Set below ground level was what appeared to be a bunker. We walked down a few steps, and as we approached the large metal door, it opened.

"Where are we going?"

"This is the underground section of the Range."

"I didn't even realise there was one."

"You wouldn't. It's not visible on open days. It only appears on advanced days."

"What's down here?"

"You'll find out soon enough. Now you're a level three witch, the single most important thing you must do is to concentrate on spell selection and customisation."

"What about focus?"

"You shouldn't even have to ask! Focus is always important. Now that you have an armoury of spells, it's essential that you are able to select the right spell for the right situation. Not only that, you need to be able to customise that spell to suit your circumstances at that moment in time. That's what today's lesson is about."

"What will I be doing, exactly?"

"There are several sections to the underground area. One of them is a sort of obstacle course."

"That sounds fun."

"We'll see if you still think so when this task is over."

She led me through a series of tunnels, and then through a set of double doors into what looked like the entrance to a concrete maze.

"What happens now?"

"Somewhere in the maze there is a pendant. When you wear it your existing powers will be enhanced."

"Where is it?"

"That's the whole point of this task. In a moment, I will say 'one, two, three, Go!' Then you will have ten minutes to find it."

"How will I know which way to go?"

"You must leave it to your inner witch to guide you."

"And that's all I have to do? Find my way to the pendant?"

She laughed. "If only it was that simple."

I had a horrible feeling I wasn't going to like this.

"There'll be a number of obstacles in your way. It's for you to select the correct spell to overcome those obstacles."

"But I—"

"One, two—"

"Grandma!"

"Three—Go!"

She pushed me into the maze. It was dark, and I could only just see where I was going. In front of me there were two tunnels—one to the left and one to the right. Instinctively, I took the left one. I'd only gone a few yards when I heard a rumbling sound behind me. I turned to see a huge, stone ball, which filled the entire width and height of the tunnel. It was coming straight for me.

If I stayed put, and used the 'power' spell, maybe I could push it back? But what if there was too much force behind it for my spell to work? It would simply crush me. Grandma had said this task was all about spell selection. I couldn't afford to wait until it was on top of me; I had to do something now.

I cast the 'shatter' spell, and the stone ball broke into a million pieces.

My heart was pounding as I carried on down the tunnel, and came to another fork. Something told me to take the right hand tunnel. I'd only taken a few steps when I saw the flames. There was a wall of fire in front of me. What should I do now? Turn back and go the other way? No, the whole point was to show that I could overcome these obstacles.

I cast the 'rain' spell, and directed the cloud over the fire. The water soon extinguished it, and I was on my way again. After only a few more yards, I was faced with a choice of three tunnels. I'd no sooner taken the centre tunnel when I heard something scrambling about on the floor. It sounded like lots of little feet. As I got closer, I could see there were scorpions everywhere.

I could have used the 'jump' spell to get over them, but in such a confined space I was afraid I might fall to the floor, and land among them. Instead, I chose the 'levitate' spell, and lifted myself just high enough to clear them, then slowly inched my way beyond them before dropping gently to the floor.

This time there were five paths to choose from! If I tried to guess, I would have only a one in five chance of getting it right. I had to trust my inner witch. Something told me to take the one second from the left. Yes, second from the left, I was sure of it.

Suddenly there was a deafening roar—a terrifying sound that scared me to death. A creature, the likes of which I'd never seen before, was running towards me. It was a kind of lion/rhinoceros hybrid with very sharp teeth and a horn on its nose. I had to act quickly. I fired a lightning bolt at it, but it just bounced off its armour-plated body. I cast the 'sleep' spell, but that had no effect. It was getting closer and closer.

I didn't have time to think, so I just acted instinctively, and made myself invisible. To my amazement and relief, the creature slowed and then stopped. It obviously didn't have much of a sense of smell, and was relying solely on sight. Although the top of its body was armour plated, the area underneath its chin and belly looked like soft skin. I cast the 'power' spell, pulled back my arm, and punched it under the jaw as hard as I could. The creature rolled backwards and fell onto its side, stunned. I wasn't sure how long I would have before it recovered, so I rushed past it as quickly as I could.

When I reached the end of the tunnel, I saw something hanging from the wall in front of me. Something gold. It was the pendant. I'd made it! I picked it up and slipped it over my head. As I did, the wall in front of me opened and there stood Grandma.

"Took you long enough, didn't it?" she said. "Come on out then."

I should have known better than to expect praise from Grandma. Once the test was over, she disappeared without so much as a 'well done'. I was absolutely exhausted as I made my way out of the Range. That's probably why I didn't notice someone creeping up behind me until it was too late.

I was sent tumbling to the floor by the push on my back.

"What the—?"

I looked up to see Alicia's side-kick, Cyril, standing over me.

"That's where you belong, Gooder." He snarled. "In the dirt."

"Where's your big sister, Cyril? Has she let you come out to play on your own?"

Under normal circumstances, I would have given the stupid little runt a kick up the backside, and sent him on his way, but I was bone-tired and could hardly think straight.

"You're finished, Gooder. Say goodbye to your pathetic little life!" He raised his hand, and I could sense he was about to fire a thunderbolt at me. I was powerless to get out of the way. Was this it? I'd always known that TDO might one day get the better of me, but it had never crossed my mind that I might die at the hands of this little pipsqueak.

I closed my eyes, and waited for the inevitable.

"Ouch! Ouch!" Cyril screamed in agony.

I opened my eyes to find him hopping around. It took me a few seconds to work out what had happened, but then I spotted the hammer which had finally returned from orbit. It had obviously landed on Cyril's foot.

I scrambled to my feet, and dusted myself down.

Cyril was groaning louder than ever.

"Serves you right." I laughed. "Now, hop it!"

Chapter 3

I'd just about recovered by the time I got back to the office. After that session at the Range, I needed some peace, quiet and sanity.

Who was I kidding?

Mrs V appeared to be shredding the Yellow Pages.

In my office, over by the leather sofa, was a huge pile of white stuff. For a moment I thought Mrs V had gone wild with the shredder again, but on closer examination, I could see that it was some kind of stuffing. The kind used in soft toys.

Just then, a pair of ears appeared above the pile of stuffing.

"Winky? Is that you behind there?"

"I'm a bit busy at the moment."

"I can see that, but what exactly are you doing?"

"What does it look like?"

"It looks like you have a mountain of stuffing."

"Your observation skills are as keen as ever."

"What are you doing with it?"

"Making soft toys, obviously."

"The soft toy market is very competitive you know. Do you think you'll actually sell any?"

"Of course. I'm not just selling *any old* soft toy. This is an exclusive line."

"Can I take a look?"

He held up one of the finished toys for me to see.

"It looks exactly like you."

"That's the whole point. It's a mini-Winky."

"Seriously though, who would want to buy one of those?"

"Hey! Just be careful what you're saying."

"I hope you haven't invested too much money in this venture. Where did you get the felt bodies from?"

"I had them manufactured overseas. They were very reasonably priced. With the mark-up I intend to add, I should make a killing."

"I don't want to pour cold water on your idea, buddy, but I'm not sure there'll be a market for these *things*."

"As always, you don't know what you're talking about. As of this morning, I have orders for over five thousand."

"*Five thousand*? Already?"

"Yes. My biggest concern is how I am going to keep pace with demand. Perhaps you could lend a hand?"

"Me?"

"Why not? It's not like you have anything else to do."

"I'll have you know I have a lot of work on at the moment."

"How many cases are you working on?"

"Err— I've lost track."

"More than one?"

"Look, I've no intention of discussing my business with you. Anyway, where are you selling these toys?"

"I've opened a new website: GetYourOwnWinky.com. If things continue like this, I'll have to bring in outside help."

"Perhaps you could get Mrs V to lend a hand?"

"The old bag lady? Not likely! She'd like to see *me* stuffed."

"That's not true."

"Of course it is. Anyway, what's with all the noise she's making out there? There's been a buzzing sound on and off all morning. Is her pacemaker playing up?"

"She's got a shredder."

"Why does she need a shredder?"

"Beats me."

"Let's just hope she doesn't have a nasty accident," he said, with a wicked grin.

"Winky. That's beneath you."

He shrugged. "I can't stand around here all day talking to you. I've got mini-Winkys to stuff, and if you're not going to help—"

"I'm not."

"Well then, the least you can do is give me some food to keep me going. Do we have any salmon?"

"Sorry, we're fresh out."

"I suppose I'll have to make do with the muck you usually serve up, then. You do have full cream milk?"

"Of course."

"Good thing too."

***

The noise from the shredder stopped about an hour later, and I could hear Mrs V talking to someone. After a few minutes, she came through to my office.

"There's a man out here asking to see you. He doesn't have an appointment."

"Who is he? What does he want?"

"I don't know. He's being very secretive. He won't tell me his name, or what he wants. I don't like him. Shall I send him away?"

"I'll see him, but give me a couple of minutes first."

Mrs V looked at the pile of partially stuffed soft toys, and shook her head.

"Winky," I shouted, once she'd left. "You'll have to shift this lot into the corner. It's going to ruin my business."

He popped his head above the pile of stuffing and laughed. "That's very funny. Like you even have a business. Why don't you work for me? I would pay you the minimum wage."

"You're so generous."

"Cash in hand."

"Look, I have a potential client out there, so I need you to move your operation into the corner so it isn't so obtrusive. Now!"

"But—"

I didn't have time for a debate with a bolshie cat, so I picked up the pile of unfinished toys and threw them into a corner.

"Hey! Watch the merchandise."

When I'd cleared as much space as I could, I went through to the outer office.

"Come through please."

The man had 'used car salesman' written all over him. From his slicked-back, obviously dyed black hair, to his pinstripe suit and black brogue shoes. And of course, the obligatory handkerchief in the breast pocket. Never trust a man with a handkerchief in his breast pocket.

"Thank you for seeing me, Miss Gooder."

"It's Jill."

"My name is Blake Devon."

He took out a business card and handed it to me. It turned out he was a lawyer. Used car salesman, lawyer? Same difference.

"How can I help you, Mr Devon?"

"Please call me Blake."

"Have a seat—Blake."

He cast an eye over the pile of soft toys, and gave me a quizzical look.

"It's a charity thing. I agreed that the local cat rescue could use part of my office to make the toys."

"I see." He obviously didn't, and who could blame him? "I represent a large multinational company. They're currently having a few issues involving the loss of certain trade secrets."

"Do they think someone is spying on them?"

"Not spying, exactly. Not anyone from outside the business, anyway. They think there may be someone on the payroll who is leaking information."

"I see."

"They would like you to investigate this matter."

"I'm afraid industrial espionage isn't really my forte." Out of the corner of my eye, I could see Winky laughing. I ignored him. "I specialise more in missing persons, infidelity, kidnapping—that sort of thing."

"You come highly recommended. And besides, my client is keen not to employ one of the larger, well-known companies because these stories have a tendency to fall into the hands of the press. We wouldn't want that, so the lower-key the better." He looked around my office. "No offence, but it doesn't get much lower-key than this."

No offence?

"Even so, Blake. I'm not sure I'll be able to help."

"Before you make a decision, I should tell you that the fee in question is very generous indeed." He took out a sheet of paper, and pushed it across the desk to me. Wow!

"But then, I am always looking to extend into other

areas. It doesn't do to get stuck in a rut," I said, still transfixed by the figure on the sheet of paper in front of me.

"I hoped you might see it that way. So, can I tell my client that you're interested in taking the case?"

"I'd certainly be prepared to discuss it in more detail."

"Excellent. That's all I can ask."

"When could I meet with your client?"

"This is a delicate situation. It wouldn't be appropriate for you to visit my client at his main office, so he'd like to hold the meeting at one of the smaller, satellite offices. That way, there would be no possibility of anyone asking any awkward questions."

"I understand."

"Excellent. Let me get back to my client and tell him the good news. I'll contact you to arrange a time and place for the meeting."

With that, he left.

"You'd sell your soul if someone offered you enough money," Winky said.

"What do you mean?"

"One minute, you don't deal with industrial matters, and the next, you're falling over yourself to take the case."

"It's important to broaden my experience."

"So, it had nothing to do with the amount of money he offered you, then?"

"Of course not. I can't be bought."

For some unknown reason, Winky was rolling around on the floor, laughing.

***

I left the office earlier than usual because I needed plenty of time to prepare for my date with Luther.

Once I was ready, and before I left my flat, I gave myself a good talking to in the mirror. Play it cool, Jill! If he tries to kiss you, act all coy and surprised. You don't want to scare him off. Got it? Got it! Okay, let's do this.

He answered the door dressed in a plain white shirt and a pair of smart trousers. A big improvement on the jogging bottoms he'd worn on our last *date*. This was beginning to look promising.

"Hi, Jill. Thanks for coming. I wasn't sure if you'd make it."

"I managed to get away from the office early."

"Come in. Would you like a drink?"

"That would be lovely. I'll have a vodka, please."

"Oh? Right. I was going to have a coffee. It's a little early—"

"Did I say vodka? I meant coffee. Thanks."

His flat was very classy. Much like mine. We were an excellent match, if I did say so myself. Things may have gone a little awry last time, but I had a good feeling about tonight.

"There you go." He put the cup on the coffee table in front of me. "You're probably wondering what the surprise is."

"The surprise? I'd forgotten all about that," I lied.

"I hope I didn't build your hopes too high."

"Not at all. I've hardly given it a thought." Only every second of every minute of every hour since he'd told me.

"Come through to the other room, and I'll show you." I didn't need telling twice. "There you are." He pointed to the table.

'There you are'? I was trying to figure out what I was meant to be looking at.

"There, on the table—look."

All I could see was a pile of booklets.

"It's my new brochure. The one you helped me to produce."

"Your brochure?"

"Yes. Here—take a look." He handed one to me. "Don't you think the printers have done an excellent job?"

"Excellent." *This* was the surprise? *This* is what I'd been building myself up for?

"I think what they've done with the cover is absolutely fantastic. Don't you agree?"

"The cover? Yeah—*fantastic*."

"Take a look inside. Your photo is in there."

I could barely summon up the enthusiasm to flick through the pages. When Kathy found out about this, my life wouldn't be worth living. How had I managed to do this to myself again? Would I ever learn? What exactly had I thought the surprise would be? Had I expected him to sweep me off my feet, and carry me into the bedroom? I had to face it—I really was delusional.

"What do you think?" he said.

"It's very nice."

"Look, there's the photo of you."

"Oh yes." I hated photos of myself.

"And look at the little speech bubble at the side where you say how much you've got from my services."

"Chance would be a fine thing!"

"Sorry?"

Had I actually said that out loud? "I was just saying, the

brochure is first class. I'm really pleased you decided to show it to me."

"That's not the only surprise, Jill."

"It isn't?" There was still hope!

"Of course not. I really want to show my gratitude for your help with this."

Now we're talking! Yes, Luther! Please show me your gratitude. I need to see your hot, sexy gratitude right now.

"I'd like to take you out for dinner. It's the least I can do. I hope you don't mind, but I've taken the liberty of booking a table."

"When for?"

"Tomorrow, if that suits you?"

Yes! Result! "That would be very nice."

See? What did I tell you? He did have feelings for me, but he wanted to wine and dine me before acting on them. I'd been right all along! The brochure had just been a ploy to get me into his flat. Now we were going out on our first real date, and I couldn't wait.

Chapter 4

Nobody made breakfast like Aunt Lucy. Porridge followed by yummy bacon, eggs, sausage and the rest. Clearly I wasn't the only one who thought so, because the twins were already seated at the kitchen table when I arrived.

They were giggling. I always worried when they giggled.

"What's going on with you two?"

"Nothing." Amber shrugged. "What makes you think there's something going on?"

"I know you two. Something's happened. What is it, Pearl?"

"Well—" she said. "It's Grandma."

That wasn't good news.

"What about her?"

"You'll never guess," Amber said.

"No, I won't. So tell me."

"It's the last thing in the world you would expect." Pearl giggled.

"If you don't tell me right now, I'm going to pour this porridge over your heads."

"No need to be so ratty." Amber pouted. "We're only having a laugh."

"So are you going to tell me or what?"

"Grandma's entering a competition."

"What kind of competition?"

"You'll never guess," Pearl said.

"We've done this already! Just tell me what kind of competition she's entering."

"A 'Glamorous Grandmother' competition."

"Oh yeah. Very funny. Seriously, what's the competition?"

"It's true!" Amber insisted. "She is, honestly."

"You two are winding me up. Just how stupid do you think I am?"

"They're not," Aunt Lucy said. "They're telling the truth."

"*A glamorous grandmother competition?*" I laughed. "Doesn't she own a mirror?"

"That's rather cruel." Aunt Lucy gave me a disapproving look. "True, but still cruel."

"She can't possibly think she stands a chance?"

"She's taking it very seriously." Aunt Lucy picked up the empty porridge bowl. "And if she is, we'd better do the same."

"How am I supposed to keep a straight face when she tells me about it?"

"You'd better try or you'll be in big trouble."

I heard the front door open.

"She's here now," Aunt Lucy said. "She said she was coming around this morning."

"Oh no. I'd better be going." I made to stand up.

"You stay right where you are." Aunt Lucy put a hand on my shoulder. "If we have to deal with this, so do you."

Betrayed by my own stomach. If I hadn't been tempted by Aunt Lucy's breakfast, I would have missed this travesty.

"Good morning, ladies," Grandma said. "And Jill."

She did it every time. She knew just how to wind me up.

"Morning, Grandma," everybody said.

"Have you told Jill my news?"

"No," the twins chorused.

Aunt Lucy shook her head.

They were doing this deliberately.

"Good. I wanted to tell her myself." She turned her evil eye on me. "You'll be pleased to hear that I've decided to enter Candlefield's Glamorous Grandmother competition."

I mustn't laugh. If I laughed, I was dead. If I laughed, she'd turn me into a frog or something even worse.

"Really?" I cleared my throat to stifle the laugh. "Sorry, I've got a bit of a cough. That's nice. When is it?"

"Don't worry. I'll let you have all the details. I expect all of you to be there to support me."

"Yes, Grandma, we'll be there," Amber said.

She was such a creep.

"Yes, we'll be there in the front row rooting for you," Pearl said.

Creeps, the pair of them.

"I'll be there, Mother," Aunt Lucy said.

They all made me sick.

"What about you, Jill?"

"I'll be there too, Grandma. I can't wait to cheer you on."

What do you mean? Who are you calling a hypocrite?

As soon as Aunt Lucy and I were alone, she said, "Have you thought any more about what I told you? About your father wanting to see you?"

I'd thought about little else since.

When I'd first learned about my family in Candlefield, I'd wrongly assumed that my father was dead. It was only later that I found out he was still alive. He'd walked out on my mother before I was born, and that had been the last anyone had seen or heard of him. I knew he'd been a very powerful wizard, but that he'd been tempted by black magic, and had fallen in with a bad crowd. Why had he come back now? And, why did he want to see me?

"Jill? What do you think?"

I'd zoned out.

"I don't want to see him."

Aunt Lucy looked surprised, but perhaps also relieved. "Are you sure?"

"Absolutely sure. I have all the family I need. I have my adoptive family in Washbridge, and I have you guys here in Candlefield. I can understand why my mother gave me up; she had good reason. But my father? Why should I see him? He never cared about me."

"Would you like more time to think about it?"

"No. Tell him I don't want to see him, and not to get in touch with me ever again."

***

Barry came bounding over as soon as I went upstairs in Cuppy C. He was back to his bubbly self.

"Can we go for a walk? Can we go now? Can we go to the park? Please, please? Can we?"

"Whoa! Steady on there. You're looking much happier than the last time I saw you."

"Oh yes. I feel great."

"How are you getting along with Hamlet?"

"We're good friends now."

"I'm really pleased to hear that."

"He reads me stories."

"He does?"

"Yes, a bedtime story, every night. At the moment he's reading me one about a giant lobster."

"That sounds — great."

"It is. It's very exciting. His name's Duke."

"Who?"

"The lobster. He's like a super hero lobster."

"Oh right. I've never heard of that book."

"You should ask Hamlet to lend it to you after he's finished reading it to me."

"I might do that."

"I have some other really exciting news." Barry was so manic that he could hardly stand still.

"What's that?"

"I have a girlfriend."

"You do?" This was news to me. "Who is she?"

"Her name's Beth."

"And where does Beth live?"

"Next door to Aunt Lucy."

"What is she?"

"She's a dog, like me."

"Yeah, I know that. I meant — never mind."

"She's beautiful. I'm in love with her."

"That's nice. And does Beth love you?"

"I don't know. I haven't spoken to her yet, but I've seen her through Aunt Lucy's bedroom window. I know she'll love me too."

"I see." This was beginning to sound a lot like my relationships.

It was nice to see Barry happy again, and really kind of

Hamlet to read to him. More surprisingly, Barry apparently now had a love interest, which was more than could be said of me. But then, I did have my dinner date with Luther to look forward to, so maybe soon Barry wouldn't be the only one with a love life.

I lived in hope.

***

I was in serious shopping mode when my phone rang.

"Oh, so you *are* still alive?" Kathy said. "I was beginning to wonder."

"I've been busy."

"I thought you might have called to let me know how you got on with Luther, and to tell me what his little surprise was."

"Like I said, I've been up to my neck in it."

"So I take it that you and he are not an item?"

"If you must know, Luther is taking me to dinner tonight."

"Well, colour me shocked."

"Oh ye of little faith."

"What was his surprise?"

"Err—the dinner date." I thought it best not to mention the brochures. "He wanted to surprise me by telling me about the dinner date."

"Where are you now?"

"In town shopping."

"You wouldn't be looking for a new outfit by any chance, would you?"

"Maybe."

"What about that little black number you bought for the

last *date*?"

"I can't wear that. Luther's already seen it. Look, did you call for anything in particular? I am rather busy."

"Excuse me for wanting to speak to my sister."

"It's just that I do have rather a lot of shopping to do, and I've got an appointment to have my hair done—and a manicure."

"Wow! You really are pushing the boat out. Let's hope you haven't read more into it than there is, this time."

"He asked me out for dinner. He's booked a table. This time it's a real date."

"Let's hope you're right."

***

In the end, I chose a rather unsubtle red number. It was an *'if you've got it, flaunt it'* type of dress. Or, in my case, *'if you've got a little bit of it, make the most of it'*.

We'd arranged to meet at the restaurant at eight o'clock. By the time I arrived, I was as nervous as a kitten. I'd had the hots for Luther ever since he'd replaced my previous accountant, Robert Roberts. It was obvious now that Luther felt the same way about me. Why else would he have asked me out to dinner? I was sure—this was going to be the start of something big.

The maître d' greeted me with a false smile.

"Good evening. Does madam have a reservation?"

"I'm meeting Mr Luther Stone."

He checked the book. "Ah yes. Mr Stone's party is over in the far corner. Follow me, please."

So Luther was already here? That was a good sign. He was obviously keen. And better still, we were in a section of the restaurant, which I could see had subdued lighting. Maybe tonight was the night, after all?

"Jill! I'm so pleased you could make it," Luther said. "Do come and join us."

Us? Do come and join *us*? He was sitting at a table with ten other people.

I forced a smile. What was going on? This was meant to be *our* dinner date.

"You probably recognise everyone?"

Sure enough, the faces were familiar. They were all people who'd posed for the photographs which had been included in Luther's brochure. This must have been his way of thanking them. Of thanking all of us. It wasn't a cosy little dinner date for two after all.

The only free chair was at the opposite end of the table from Luther. As I took my seat, I noticed that the young woman sitting next to him *wasn't* someone from the brochure. The last time I'd seen her was when she and Luther had come to my flat. It was *Loo – sin – da*, and she looked awfully friendly with Luther.

"Waiter!" I called. "Get me a vodka. Make it a large one!"

Chapter 5

When I woke the next morning, I wondered for a moment if the *dinner date that wasn't* had just been a bad dream. I quickly realised that it had been only too real. It had been bad enough having to make small talk with ten total strangers, but the worst part had been having to watch Lucinda flirting with Luther all night long.

Oh, well. He'd had his chance and he'd blown it. I was done with him.

The last time I'd seen my neighbour, Mr Ivers, he'd been depressed, but this morning, there'd been a total transformation. The man was smiling from ear to ear.

"Jill! Hello! Isn't it a beautiful day?"

It was cold and raining, but I didn't see any reason to dampen his spirits. "You're looking very pleased with life."

"I am, and it's all down to you."

"Really? What did I do?"

"Don't be so modest. I have you to thank for referring me to Love Spell."

I'd forgotten all about that. Mr Ivers had been so down because he didn't have a girlfriend that I'd suggested he join the Love Spell dating agency. It was an agency which specialised in matching witches from Candlefield with human men from Washbridge. At the time, I'd thought maybe I'd made a mistake, and that the girls from Love Spell would be annoyed that I'd referred boring Mr Ivers to them. Far from it; they'd been quite happy to have him on their books. According to them, there was quite a demand for movie buffs among the female witch population. Who knew?

"How's that going? Have you been on any dates?"

"Only one, but I'm pleased to report that it was a great success. I've actually met my special *someone*! We've been out together a couple of times."

Unbelievable. How come I couldn't get a date for love nor money, but Mr Ivers, the most boring man in the world, had hit it off first time. Not that I was bitter. Not in the least.

"Her name is Wendy; she loves the movies."

No real surprises there.

"She has a fantastic knowledge of the cinema for a woman."

Oh dear — please don't say that to her — ever!

"She really knows her stuff. Anyway, I'm pleased that I've bumped into you. I was thinking maybe Wendy and I could go on a double date with you and — err — what's the name of the man you're dating?"

Good question. "I'm afraid I'm rather busy at the moment, Mr Ivers. I've got a lot of cases on. I'm not sure I'll be able to make it for the foreseeable future."

"That's a shame. Wendy would love to meet you."

"And I'd love to meet her, but like I said. I'm jammed with work at the moment."

"I'm sure you'll like her, Jill. I call her my lucky charm."

"Why's that?"

"It's really strange. Ever since we've been together, everything seems to be going my way. The other day, for example, we went out together to the local park. It was really hot and sticky, and I mentioned to Wendy that I was feeling quite uncomfortable in the heat. And then, the strangest thing happened: a single rain cloud appeared above my head, and it started to rain. The curious thing was that it didn't seem to rain on anyone else. I mean, what were the chances of that happening?"

"That's amazing." And it sounded very much like magic to me. Didn't Wendy realise that she wasn't meant to let her human dates know she was a witch?

"And another strange thing happened. You know how I love liquorice allsorts?"

"I didn't actually know that."

"Oh, yes. I adore them. The other day we were watching a movie, and I could have sworn I'd eaten the last one. I was just about to say I wished we'd bought more of them when the bag was suddenly full again! Wendy said I must have been mistaken."

"Yeah, that must have been it." Or, more likely, Wendy had used the 'take it back' spell.

"Since I met Wendy, things seem to have clicked into place. So, I just wanted to thank you."

"My pleasure, Mr Ivers. I'm pleased I could help."

And off he went on his merry way, whistling as he went. Maybe I should have a quiet word with Wendy before she overstepped the mark, and got picked up by the Rogue Retrievers?

***

Mrs V appeared to be pulling at her desk as though she was trying to stand up.

"Mrs V, are you all right?"

"Yes, dear. I'm fine."

As I stepped closer, I could see that she was handcuffed to the desk.

"What happened? Has someone tried to rob us?"

"No. Why would you think that, dear?"

"You're handcuffed to the desk!"

"Oh that? I did it."

"Why would you handcuff yourself to the desk?"

"It's the only way I can stop myself."

"From doing what?"

"Shredding. It's like an addiction. I can't help myself."

In my crazy world, I'd come across many weird and wonderful things, but an addiction to shredding had caught even me on the hop.

"I was worried that I'd shred something of vital importance," she said. "So I thought I'd better handcuff myself to the desk. Do you think there's a name for what I have?"

"I'm pretty sure there is."

"Really? What is it?"

"Crazy!"

"You have to help me. Maybe there's some sort of support group I could join?"

"You mean like 'Shredders Anonymous'?"

"Yes, they might be able to help. Would you check and see if there's a local group?"

"No problem. I'll do it now." I took the Yellow Pages from the bottom drawer of the filing cabinet. Half the pages were missing—presumably they'd been shredded. I flicked through until I found what I was looking for, and made a call.

"Thank you, Jill. When is the next meeting?"

"There isn't a meeting."

"But I thought you were calling Shredders Anonymous?"

"No. I had a better idea. I called a used office equipment company. They're going to come and take away the machine."

"No! You can't let them do that!"

She made a grab for the key to the handcuffs, but I snatched it away.

"Please, Jill, don't take the machine away."

"You'll thank me later." Sometimes you have to be cruel to be kind.

The men who came to collect the stupid machine must have thought Mrs V was some kind of nutjob when they saw her handcuffed to the desk, screaming at them not to take her beloved shredder.

***

I heard voices in the outer office. A few moments later, Mrs V, now minus the handcuffs, popped her head around my door.

"Jill, I'm sorry to trouble you. I know you're busy, but there are three women out here. They don't have an appointment, but they'd like to see you if you have the time."

"Did they say who they are?"

She walked in and pushed the door closed behind her. "They won't give me their names or say what it's about, but there's something rather strange about them."

"Strange how?"

"Well, for a start, they're wearing identical drape coats. They look like secret agents of some kind."

"Do they look dangerous?"

"Definitely not. They seem rather nervous actually.

What shall I do? Shall I tell them to go away?"

I had nothing better to do, and besides, the three timid women in drape coats might actually have a job for me. It would be foolish to send them away without even speaking to them.

"Send them in, Mrs V."

"If you're sure, dear."

Just as Mrs V had said, the women were all wearing identical coats. Not only that, they'd had their hair done in the same style: a short bob cut. One was a brunette, one a blonde, and the other had jet-black hair.

"Thanks for seeing us, Ms Gooder," the one in the centre said.

"Please, call me Jill."

"I hope you don't mind us dropping in without an appointment."

"Not at all." By now, I'd realised that they were witches. "Is there something I can help you with? Do you need my services?"

"Not exactly. Let me introduce us. I'm Brenda, this is Peggy, and this is Ashley. Together, we are *The Coven*."

"The Coven?"

"That's right, The Coven."

"And what exactly is The Coven?"

Brenda beamed. "I'm glad you asked." She turned to the others. "Right girls, are you ready?" They nodded, and from somewhere, Brenda took out what appeared to be an iPod, put it on the sofa, and pressed 'play'. The three of them threw off their coats to reveal sparkly leotards. Brenda was in red, Peggy in yellow, and Ashley in blue. Then on a cue from Brenda, they began to dance.

I was mesmerised. They had obviously choreographed

their routine very carefully. After a couple of minutes, they all crouched down on one knee. I thought they'd finished, but then Brenda stood up and said, "We!"

Then Peggy jumped to her feet and said, "Are!"

Finally, Ashley leaped up and said, "The Coven!"

At that point, the music stopped. I wasn't sure if I should applaud or not.

"That was very good, thank you. But I still don't really understand why you're here."

"We know that you've been searching for The Dark One."

"I have, although I haven't made much progress."

"No one ever seems to, but we're determined that we shall find and destroy TDO," Brenda said, much more seriously now.

"Really? The three of you?"

"That's why we're here. We're hoping to persuade you to join The Coven."

"Me?" That was the last thing I'd been expecting her to say. "What exactly have you done so far in your fight against TDO, and what would my role be?"

"So far we've spent most of our time on choreography. I'd like to think it's paid dividends." The other two nodded their agreement.

"Your dance routine was very well-executed," I said. "But have you done anything in particular with regard to TDO?"

"That's next on the agenda. We wanted to get the choreography right first. But we feel we need a fourth person in the group, so we immediately thought of you, didn't we, girls?"

"That's right." Peggy nodded.

"Yes, absolutely," Ashley said. "We've seen you in The Candle."

Brenda continued. "We'd be delighted if you would join us, Jill. You could, of course, choose whichever colour leotard you like, but we'd prefer it didn't clash."

"And was there anything specific you had in mind for me to do?"

"Well, we thought you could do the 'The'.

"The 'The'?"

"Yes, at the moment I do the 'We', Peggy does the 'Are', but Ashley has to do 'The Coven'. It doesn't really work. We thought if you came on board, then I could do the 'We', Peggy could do the 'Are', you could do the 'The', and that would leave Ashley to do just the 'Coven'. It would work so much better."

"Right, I see. So I'd be the 'The'?"

"That's right."

"Look, I really appreciate you coming in today, and I'm very excited by your offer. But I am rather busy, so I'm going to have to give it some thought. Could I get back to you?"

"Of course. Let me give you a card."

Peggy reached inside the pocket of her coat, pulled out a small business card and passed it to me. Sure enough, printed on there in bright red letters was 'The Coven', together with a phone number.

"Right. Well, I'll get back to you, then."

The three women put their coats on, and left.

"Are any of the people who come to see you not insane?" Winky said.

"I'm beginning to think not."

Chapter 6

I'd arranged to meet Kathy at the local community hall where the yoga class was being held. All I really wanted was a quiet night in. Just me, a good book, lots of chocolate and a bottle of ginger beer. Instead, I had to cavort around like some kind of imbecile, just to satisfy my sister's whim.

"All set?" Kathy said, as she greeted me at the door.

"Not really."

"Come on, Jill. You'll feel much better afterwards."

"Where do we get changed into our leotards?"

"There aren't any changing rooms here. It's just a community hall. Didn't I mention that you should have your leotard on under your clothes?"

"No. You didn't *actually* mention that. Where are the toilets?"

"They're outside. Across the yard."

"I can't go out there — it's windy and raining!"

"Go into that corner. I'll hold up a towel as a screen while you get changed."

"It doesn't look like I have much choice."

It wasn't exactly the best attended event I'd ever been to. Apart from Kathy and me, there were just three other women. Two of them were at least seventy years old. This was going to be a very long evening.

"Right, ladies. Are we all ready?" the instructor shouted. I recognised the voice, and looked up to see Daze; she looked fantastic in her leotard.

"We'll start with a few gentle exercises to get you warmed up."

As with most of the roles that Daze took on, she was of course, an expert. The same could not have been said for me. I tried to follow her lead, but had great difficulty copying her movements. While everyone else seemed to cope effortlessly, I was just a mass of arms and legs flailing around.

"Jill. Here—let me help you." The voice came from behind me. I looked around to see Blaze, Daze's young sidekick. He too was wearing a leotard, but he definitely didn't look anywhere near as good as Daze.

"Do what I do, and you'll be fine." He took a step forward so he was standing just in front of me, and then went through the movements very slowly so I could follow.

"How long has Daze been teaching yoga?"

"We've been at this for about a week now. I don't really like it. I enjoyed the Punch and Judy far more."

By the time the hour was up, I was exhausted and ached everywhere.

"That was great!" Kathy said. "We should come again. What do you think, Jill?"

"I'll get back to you on that," I said, trying to straighten my back.

"Do you want to come back to our place for supper?"

"No thanks. I'll give it a miss. I'm really tired. You shoot off."

"Are you sure?"

"Positive."

"By the way, you haven't forgotten that Lizzie wants to spend a day with you in the office, have you?"

"No. I've just had a lot on. Mostly involving shredding

machines."

"Shredding machines?"

"It's a long story, but it's all resolved now. I'll give you a call to let you know when Lizzie can come."

The community hall was now empty except for Daze, Blaze and me.

"Did you enjoy that, Jill?" Daze said.

"Not really. It wasn't my idea to come. Kathy dragged me here—you might have guessed. Anyway, what are you two working on at the moment?"

"We're on the trail of a shape-shifter," Daze said.

"Another werewolf?"

"Not this time. We've had reports that a shape-shifter has been getting into people's houses here in Washbridge, and stealing their jewellery. He's doing it in the guise of a rat."

That rang a bell. I waited for her to continue.

"In fact," she said. "It's quite a clever ploy. Somehow he's managed to get himself a gig at a school. The kids apparently take it in turns to take the rat home with them to look after it for the night. The crafty shifter then takes the opportunity to raid jewellery boxes in the homes where he's staying. But we're struggling to track him down at the moment."

"I might just be able to help you there. I need to check a couple of things first, then I'll get back to you."

***

The next morning, I overslept. When I did eventually wake, I could hardly move. Every muscle in my body ached. Whoever thought yoga was a good idea? Never again! If Kathy wanted to carry on with it, she'd have to go by herself.

My phone rang. It was her. She probably wanted to check how I was, and to have a laugh at my expense.

"I ache everywhere." I moaned.

"Jill!" she screamed, and I knew immediately that something was wrong.

"What's happened?"

"It's so horrible—"

"Are Peter and the kids okay?"

"Yeah, we're all okay."

"What's wrong then?"

"It's the colonel. He's dead."

I had to sit down. I hadn't known the colonel for long, but in the short time since I'd first met him, we'd become firm friends. I'd worked on a case for him, and then he'd taken on Peter, my brother-in-law, as his gardener.

"What happened?" Although the colonel had always seemed fit, he was no spring chicken, so I assumed he must have had a heart attack or something similar.

"I don't know. Pete just rang and told me. He says the colonel was murdered."

"What?" I yelled into the phone. "Are you sure?"

"That's what Pete said."

"Where is Peter now?"

"He's still there—at the colonel's house."

"Look—I'd better speak to Peter. I'll call you back later."

I ended the call, and immediately rang Peter.

"It's Jill. Kathy just told me about the colonel."

"It's terrible."

"What happened?"

"I don't really know. He was dead when I found him. Someone murdered him, Jill."

"How?"

"He was shot with a crossbow bolt. There's blood everywhere."

"Where was he when you found him?"

"In the toy room."

"Has someone called the police?"

"Yes, they're on their way."

"Whatever you do, don't touch anything."

"It's a bit late for that."

"What do you mean?"

"When I saw the bolt, I grabbed it. I was just acting on instincts."

"Did you pull it out?"

"No. I just put my hand on it."

"Well, don't touch anything else. I'm coming over."

***

I called Mrs V.

"It's Jill. I'm not going to be in this morning. Would you feed Winky for me, please?"

"You know I hate that cat."

"The colonel's dead."

"What? Oh no! That's terrible."

I probably should have broken the news to her a little more gently. Mrs V had become quite fond of the colonel.

"What happened?" I could hear the shock in her voice.

"I don't know. I'm going over there now to try to find out."

"Don't worry about the cat. I'll see to him. Will you let me know when you have any more information?"

"Yes, of course. I'm hoping to get into the office later this morning."

Next, I made a call to Blake Devon. I told him that I wouldn't be able to take the industrial sabotage case, and I explained why. He wasn't very happy, but I didn't care. Right now my priority was finding out who had murdered the colonel.

***

When I arrived at the colonel's house there was a cordon around the place, and two uniformed officers at the gate.

"I'm sorry, madam," the officer with large ears and a very small nose said. "You can't go in there. There's been an incident."

"Detective Maxwell is expecting me," I lied.

"What's your name?"

"Jill Gooder."

"Wait there a moment." He walked back to his colleague. They exchanged a few words, and then one of them made a call on his radio. I had no idea whether they'd let me through or not. Jack Maxwell could blow hot and cold. If he was in a bad mood, he'd probably deny even knowing me. On the other hand, he knew of my connection to the colonel and Peter, so just maybe I'd be lucky.

The next thing I knew I was being waved through the gates. Maxwell had come through for me on this occasion.

When I reached the front door, Jack Maxwell was

waiting for me.

"You know you shouldn't be here," he said.

"Oh come on, Jack. What did you expect me to do? Peter found him, and you know the colonel and I were close."

"I know. That's why I allowed you through. Even so, I don't want you getting in the way. You can talk to Peter, but that's all."

"Where is he?"

"He's in one of the reception rooms, but you'll have to wait until I've finished with him. Why don't you go through to the kitchen, and wait in there? I'll let you know as soon as we're done."

"Can I sit in on the interview?"

"Don't push your luck."

I walked down the hallway, and past the toy room, which had yellow tape across the doorway. Inside, I could see men in white coveralls—obviously scene of crime officers. I was devastated to think that the colonel was dead. He was such a kind man; he'd been very generous to me and Peter. Who would have wanted to murder him? I had to find out what had happened. I didn't care what Maxwell said—I was going to get to the bottom of this.

Mrs Burnbridge, the colonel's housekeeper, had obviously been crying. She was sitting at the kitchen table with a half-empty mug of tea in front of her. She didn't even notice me walk into the room.

"Mrs Burnbridge?"

"Oh hello, dear. I didn't hear you come in. Would you like a drink?"

"It's okay. You stay where you are. I can make myself a

drink."

"No, dear. That's my job."

"Not today, Mrs Burnbridge. You've had a nasty shock."

"It's terrible. I can't believe the colonel's gone."

"Did you hear or see anything?"

"Nothing at all."

I made myself a mug of tea, and put plenty of sugar in it. After the shock of the colonel's murder, I needed something sweet.

"Does he have any family apart from his son?"

"No, only Ben. He rarely visits though. They don't get on. I'm not really sure what went wrong, but the colonel hardly ever talks about him. He did stay the night a few days ago while the colonel was away. Mind you, the only reason he came was because he was visiting a friend in the area. He treats this place like a hotel. He didn't get back in until the early hours. I was in bed, but I heard him come in. It must have been two or three o'clock in the morning. It's terrible the way he treats his father and this house. Still, I suppose I should let him know what has happened."

"I'm sure the police will do that. There's no need for you to worry your head about it."

"I just feel like I should be doing something. I feel so useless."

"No one would expect you to do anything at a time like this. Stay here and finish your tea. The police will no doubt want to talk to you at some point."

We sat in silence for a little while, and then Peter walked in.

"How are you?" I said.

"Not great."

"Do you want me to give you a lift home?"

"No, it's okay. I've got the car."

"Are you sure you're okay to drive?"

"Yeah. I'm a bit shaken, but I'm okay."

"What did the police have to say?"

"Just what you'd expect. They asked me how I found him, and whether I'd seen or heard anything."

"And did you?"

"No. Nothing at all. I had absolutely no idea anything was wrong. The colonel always has his breakfast brought to him in the toy room at about eight o'clock. But when Mrs Burnbridge took it to him this morning, he didn't answer the door."

"That's right," Mrs Burnbridge chipped in. "He always keeps the toy room door locked so as not to be disturbed. When there was no answer, I went upstairs to check if he'd overslept, but he wasn't in his bedroom. So I came back downstairs and knocked again, but there was still no reply. That's when I fetched Peter."

"I knocked too," Peter said, "And I shouted to him, but he didn't answer, so I used my key. And there he was—lying on the floor—in a pool of blood."

Chapter 7

Back at the office, Mrs V was waiting anxiously for news.

As I brought her up to speed with events, I could see the colour drain from her face. She and the colonel had developed quite a rapport in the short time she'd known him.

"How's Peter taking it?" she said.

"Not good, as you can imagine. He was the one who found him."

"And the colonel was definitely murdered?"

"It seems that way."

"But who would want to kill him?"

"I don't know, but I intend to find out."

Just then, the outer door opened, and a little head popped around it. It was Gertie. I'd helped her to sort out some of the teething problems she'd been having at her new school after she moved from Candlefield to Washbridge. The last time I'd seen her, she'd made a new friend, and seemed much more positive about living in Washbridge. But as she was here again, I could only assume that meant there was a problem.

"Come in, Gertie."

She was smiling, so maybe things weren't so bad after all. As she walked in, I realised she wasn't alone. Following behind her were Holly and Juniper, the two girls who'd been in on her faked disappearance.

"Hello, girls. Nice to see you all again. Nobody disappeared today, I hope? Why don't you come through to my office?"

"Would you like a scarf or some socks girls?" Mrs V said, as we passed by her desk.

"Perhaps they could choose some on their way out, Mrs V."

The three of them made a fuss of Winky, who of course lapped up the attention.

"I like him," Holly said. "But, why has he only got one eye?"

"He lent the other one to someone," I quipped.

"Really?"

"Of course not, Holly." Juniper laughed. "How stupid are you? Jill's only joking."

"I knew that." Holly blushed.

Gertie rolled her eyes. "See what I have to put up with?"

"How are you settling into the human world?" I asked.

"I'm having a great time. I'm really glad I decided to move to Washbridge."

"That's good to hear."

"It's so easy to make fools of humans using magic. We're having a lot of fun, aren't we girls?"

Oh dear. That didn't sound good.

"We use the 'illusion' spell to make people think they've seen things. We scared a woman with a snake. Didn't we Juniper?"

"Yeah. That was so funny!"

"Then we froze a man's dog. He thought it had turned into a statue. Didn't he, Holly?"

"Yeah, that was hilarious!"

"Girls, that's not really what you should be doing. You've got to be careful. You can't let humans know that you're performing magic."

"We reversed the spells really quickly. They just thought they'd imagined it. Anyway, we can always use the 'forget' spell if we have to."

"What about school? Is that going okay?"

"Yeah, more or less," Gertie said.

"More or less? What does that mean?"

"Well, I may have overdone the magic a little."

"How do you mean, *a little*?"

"I played a few tricks on the teacher. I used the 'move' spell on the board marker just as she was going to pick it up. Then I used the 'illusion' spell to make her think there was a rat running around her feet. Then—"

"You're supposed to keep your magic under wraps."

"Yeah, but it was so funny."

"It won't be funny if a Rogue Retriever takes you back to Candlefield."

Suddenly, Gertie looked worried.

"They wouldn't do that, would they?"

"That's their job. Rogue Retrievers are on the lookout for sups who are abusing their magical powers in the human world. Playing tricks on teachers for no good reason probably falls into that category. Do your parents know?"

"Well, they did get called into school one day because the teacher was convinced that I'd had something to do with moving the board marker. She just couldn't figure out what."

"And what did your parents have to say about it?"

"They weren't very pleased, but I told them you'd said it was okay."

"What? That's not what I said!"

"Yes, you did. You said: *You're not allowed to let humans*

know you're a witch, but there are still lots of ways to use magic without them finding out.

Had I really said that? I had a horrible feeling that I might have done.

"Is that what you told your parents?"

"Yeah."

Oh boy. I was in trouble.

***

By the end of the day, I'd gotten precisely nowhere with the colonel's murder. I needed to speak to Peter again, but this time away from the colonel's house, so I wouldn't have to worry about Jack Maxwell overhearing.

As soon as I arrived at Kathy's, she took the kids upstairs, and left Peter and me to talk.

"The colonel often spent time in his toy room in the mornings," he said. "He was like a big kid really. He loved those toys. He was particularly excited because he'd just bought a new one."

"You mean the jack-in-the-box?"

"Yeah. How did you know about that?"

"He brought it into my office a while back, but it was broken."

"He had it repaired somewhere. I heard it cost him a small fortune. The first I knew something was wrong was when Mrs Burnbridge came to fetch me from the garden. She couldn't get in to give the colonel his breakfast."

"Did he usually lock the door?"

"Yeah, I don't really know why. I think maybe he was a bit embarrassed by his hobby, but also he didn't like to be disturbed. Mrs Burnbridge took him breakfast at the same time each morning. But today he didn't answer when she knocked. When I got there, there was no sound from inside the room. I knew something was wrong."

"Why doesn't Mrs Burnbridge have a key?"

"She usually does, but the colonel lost his a while back, so he was using hers until he could get another one cut."

"Was he already dead when you got inside the room?"

"I think so. There was so much blood. It was horrible."

"What did you do?"

"Like I told the police, it's all a bit of a blur. I can remember kicking the jack-in-the-box out of the way. He must have been holding it when he was shot. Then I bent over him to check if he was still alive—that's when I touched the bolt. I'm not sure if I called the police, or if Mrs Burnbridge did. They arrived soon after. Since then I've been answering questions. Sorry, Jill, but I need a shower and then I'm going to lie down for a while. I'm shattered."

"Sure. I understand. You go ahead."

He disappeared upstairs, and shortly after, Kathy came into the kitchen followed by Lizzie.

"Pete will be okay," she said. "It's just the shock."

"Yeah, I know."

"Auntie Jill." Lizzie tugged at my arm. "When am I going to go to work with you for the day?"

"Err—soon, Lizzie. I've just got one or two things to sort out first."

"Because some of the other kids have already done it."

"Don't worry. I haven't forgotten you. I'll clear a day, and we'll arrange something."

Mikey walked in and began to bang his drum.

"Mikey, not today!" Kathy shouted.

"But, Mum, I'm getting really good—"

"I said, not today. Put it away in your bedroom now."

Mikey pulled a sulky face, and headed upstairs to his bedroom.

"Oh, by the way," I said. "Has any of your jewellery or other items gone missing?"

"Not that I'm aware of. Why?"

"I heard that several people with children at the same school as yours have had jewellery stolen."

"It's funny you should mention that, because a few mothers did say they'd had jewellery go missing, but I'm not sure if they bothered to report it. It was just the odd bracelet or a pair of earrings. They more or less decided they must have misplaced them."

"Do they still have that rat at school?"

"Since when do you care about the rat?"

"I just thought it was unusual for a school to keep a rat, that's all."

"As far as I know, they do."

What's this all about, Jill?"

"Nothing. Just making conversation."

Note to self: let Daze know that she'll find her rogue shifter at Mikey and Lizzie's school.

***

I *had* thought Betty Longbottom was a pleasant young woman. A bit boring maybe, but then she was a tax inspector. But I'd been wrong. She was dangerous; downright dangerous. Just because she'd seen me with

Luther, she'd put a jellyfish outside my front door!

If she thought I was going to speak to her after that, she could think again. I would just walk straight past her.

"Jill, do you have a minute?"

"I'm rather busy at the moment, Betty."

"Jill, please. Could I just have a word? I'm really, really sorry about what I did. I don't know what came over me. I think it was the green-eyed monster. I can't think why else I would have done something so horrible."

"It's not like you have anything to be jealous about, Betty. Luther and I aren't seeing each other." Not yet anyway. Maybe soon, but I didn't need to tell *her* that.

"I know. It's just that—well, I had thought maybe I had a chance with him. Then, when I saw you with him, I realised that he didn't like me after all. I just lost the plot, but I should never have done it. Are you okay?"

"The sting was really painful."

"I know. I feel terrible. Please let me make it up to you."

"That's really not necessary."

"Please, I want to. I'd like to give you a little present."

"Don't be silly. You don't need to do that."

"Please, Jill. It would make me feel so much better if you allowed me to."

"Well, okay then."

"That's great. Come with me, I've actually got something for you already."

"You have?"

"I've got a selection of things actually. I thought maybe you could pick your own present."

Now I was confused. Did she have a present for me or not? What was going on? I was curious enough to follow her. Once inside her flat, we headed to the spare bedroom.

Holy moly, it was like an Aladdin's cave! The room was piled high with all manner of expensive perfumes, designer handbags, designer shoes and jewellery. It must have been worth a small fortune!

"Where did all this come from, Betty?"

"I love to shop, but I often end up buying things which I don't really need. Everything in here is brand new. I'm not trying to fob you off with my cast-offs. Would you like a handbag?"

"No, I'm okay for handbags, thanks."

"Some shoes, then?"

I glanced at her clodhopper feet. "I don't think you and I are the same size."

"What about some jewellery?"

"I couldn't possibly accept jewellery. Maybe some perfume though, if that's okay?"

"Yes, of course. Help yourself. I have lots to choose from."

She was right. She had a bigger selection than most of the shops in town. I picked one of the more expensive ones.

"I really am sorry, Jill. Have you forgiven me?"

"Yes, of course. We all do stupid things from time to time." Me more than most.

At least I'd got a bottle of perfume out of the deal. A really nice one too. Maybe Luther would like it.

When I got back to my flat, my mother's ghost appeared. She wasn't alone.

"Hi, Alberto."

"Good to see you, Jill. Long time, no see."

"You too. How are you?"

"Okay thanks."

Apart from the small matter of being dead, obviously.

"Did you come for some custard creams, Mum?"

She blushed under Alberto's glare. Oh dear, I might have just dropped her in it. Snigger.

"Of course not. You know I don't eat those any more, Jill." She stared pointedly at me. "I've cut them out completely, haven't I, Alberto?"

"I thought you had."

"Anyway, that's not why we're here," my mother said, desperately trying to change the subject. "We have some news. Alberto and I have decided to take a belated honeymoon."

"Really? That's nice. Where are you going?"

"We've decided on a cruise."

"Is that possible? For ghosts I mean?"

"Of course. Why wouldn't it be?"

"Won't it be expensive?"

"Not for ghosts, no."

I must have looked a little puzzled because she went on to explain. "We don't need to buy tickets. We can just glide on board the ship."

"So, you'll be stowaways?"

"I'm not sure I'd use the term stowaway."

"What would you call yourselves?"

"VIP passengers." She laughed. "We'll be staying in one of the better suites."

"What about the people who've already paid for that accommodation?"

"They won't mind. They won't even know we're there. They might think the room is a little cold, and we'll have to be careful not to knock things over, but other than that, they won't be any the wiser. I'm just a little worried about leaving you here alone. I'm normally close by, so if you have any problems, I can get to you quickly."

"Can't ghosts just travel through the ether?" I said.

"What's the ether?"

"I've no idea. It's just something I've heard people say. I assumed that ghosts could move around at the speed of light."

"It's not as simple as that. Normally, we can move around fairly quickly, but not when we have to travel over water."

"Why's that?"

"Water and ghosts?" she said. "Not a good mix. Once we're on the ship, it'll be more difficult to get back."

"Don't worry about me. I can look after myself. I'm a level three witch now remember."

"I know, but there are still evil powers with their eyes on you. You know that you can always call on your Aunt Lucy or Grandma, don't you?"

"Of course. Don't worry about me. Go and enjoy your honeymoon."

"If there *was* some kind of dire emergency," my mother said. "There are ways in which I could get back quicker, even with the water. But it's a bit complicated, and it would need you to have a word with your friend, Madeline."

"With Mad? How could she help?"

"You know what she does, I take it?"

"I know she's doing similar work to a Rogue Retriever. Bringing back rogue ghosts from the human world."

"That's right. But she also has an 'in' with the people in authority in Ghost Town, and if there was an emergency, she could speak to someone to arrange special transport for Alberto and me."

"I'm sure that won't be necessary."

"You're probably right. But I just wanted you to know that if the worst came to the worst, you do have that option. If there is a problem, talk to Madeline."

"Okay. When are you going?"

"Straight away. The ship sets sail later tonight."

"Well, have a lovely honeymoon."

"We will. We'll bring you back a present."

Chapter 8

When I arrived at the office the next morning, Mrs V was still suffering from SWS (Shredder Withdrawal Symptoms). She was staring longingly into the empty corner of the room where the shredder had been.

"Are you okay, Mrs V?"

"I will be, in time. It might take me a while to get over it."

"Did you feed Winky this morning?"

"I can't get into your office."

"What do you mean?"

"The door won't open."

"You don't think he's lying dead behind the door, do you?"

She shrugged. Mrs V was far more concerned about the missing shredder than she was about Winky.

I hurried over to the door. She was right, so I put my shoulder to it, and pushed as hard as I could. Eventually, I managed to get it open far enough to squeeze through. Then I saw why I hadn't been able to get in. The floor and every surface was covered with mini-Winkys. Over by the window, there was some kind of production line where five cats were stuffing yet more of them.

Winky was perched on my desk, overseeing his workforce. I had to pick my way carefully across the room, to avoid standing on any of the toys.

"What on earth is going on here?"

"Isn't it obvious? Even to you?"

"Why are there a thousand mini-Winkys all over the floor?"

"I think you'll find there are two thousand, one

hundred and sixty-five. At the last count."

"Whatever. What are they doing here? This is my office. How am I meant to work with all this going on?"

"You worry too much. Take a seat. Suck on a mint."

I managed to step over the last few toys in my path, and slumped down in the chair. "This can't continue. And what are all these other cats doing here? How did they get in?"

"I have my methods."

"Where did they come from?"

"The job centre, of course."

"Since when did the job centre cater for cats?"

"Not the human job centre! The feline job centre. They're only temporary. I have them on a fixed term contract. I'm paying them as little as possible," he whispered.

"I might have known. Look, this venture of yours is obviously hugely successful, although goodness knows how. You can't continue to run it out of my office. You'll have to find alternative premises. Can't you rent an industrial unit somewhere? There are some to let near the park."

"That won't be necessary. It's all in hand."

"In hand how?"

"I've just agreed to licence mini-Winky to one of the large toy manufacturers. As from tomorrow, they'll take over the manufacture, sales and distribution. And I'll get a royalty for every toy sold. Sounds like a sweet deal to me."

"And what's my cut?"

He laughed. "Why would you get a cut?"

"For funding your start-up by providing you with

somewhere to work."

"In your dreams."

***

It was useless trying to work out of my office. I'd given Winky an ultimatum to get his workforce and all of the mini-Winkys out of there by the end of business, or I would dispose of them myself. I wasn't sure he believed me, but I was deadly serious. I wasn't going to let a cat push me around. What? Who are you calling a pushover?

As I made my way out of the office, I put my heel through one of the toys.

Whoops!

"Hey! Be careful," Winky shouted after me. "I'll bill you for damages!"

"Good luck with that."

"Is he dead?" Mrs V said, quite uninterested.

"No, he's alive and well. I'd forgotten that I had a clear-out yesterday, and left some stuff on the floor. I wouldn't bother going in there for the rest of the day."

"Is it my imagination, or is he meowing more than usual?"

"I don't think so."

I thought it best not to tell her that there were another five cats next door.

My phone rang; it was Peter.

"Jill, you said I should let you know if there were any developments."

"What's happened?"

"I've just arrived at the colonel's house. His son is here. I thought you would want to know."

"I'll pop over there now. Maybe I can grab a word with him."

When I arrived at the house, I was greeted by Mrs Burnbridge. The two of us joined Peter in the kitchen.

"Would you like a cup of tea, dear?"

"Yes please, Mrs Burnbridge."

"Peter tells me that you're rather particular about your sugar."

I glared at him. "Not really. I just like one and two thirds teaspoons."

She gave me a sympathetic look. Why did people have such a problem with my insistence on precision when it came to sweetener?

Mrs Burnbridge had a selection of muffins, and even though it wasn't long since I'd had breakfast, I didn't want to appear rude, so I took a blueberry one.

"I hear the colonel's son has turned up."

"Like a bad penny," she said.

"How well do you know him?"

"I've met him a few times. When the colonel did talk about him, which wasn't often, I got the impression that his son was a bit of a disappointment. But he's quick enough to show his face now his father is dead, I see." The disgust was obvious in her voice. "Anyway, it doesn't matter to me. There's no reason for me to stay on now the colonel's gone. I should have retired years ago, but I couldn't bring myself to leave him on his own. You know what men are like. They can't cope without us women, can they?"

"That's true. So what will you do now?"

"I have a few hobbies. I enjoy knitting."

"Really? You should talk to my P.A. You may have heard of her: Annabel Versailles?"

"Annabel? Of course, everyone knows Annabel. She's something of a celebrity in knitting circles. I didn't realise she worked for you."

"She doesn't exactly *work* for Jill," Peter butted in. "Or at least she does, but Jill doesn't pay her."

"Take no notice of him, Mrs Burnbridge." I shot Peter a look. "Annabel and I have an arrangement. It's all above board. So when do you intend to leave?"

"I'll stay around until after the reading of the colonel's Will, and then I'll leave Benjamin to it."

"Where is Ben, anyway?" I said.

"The last time I saw him, he was in the toy room. The police have finished in there now. I think he was looking around to see what he could sell. I'm pretty sure he'll want to offload the house and all the contents."

"Are the toys worth anything?"

"I believe some of them are quite valuable. In fact, the man who took away the jack-in-the-box for repair made the colonel an offer for it. But the colonel said it wasn't for sale."

I finished my tea and muffin, and then went in search of the colonel's son. It didn't take me long to find him; he was still in the toy room. The door was ajar, so I knocked and walked in.

"Who are you?" he said, stony-faced.

"I'm Jill Gooder. I was a friend of your father's."

"Oh, right. Did you want something?"

"I did some work for your father; I'm a private investigator. My brother-in-law, Peter, is the gardener here."

"Yes? And how can I help you?"

"Actually, I may be able to help you. I know the police are investigating your father's death, but I wondered if you'd like me to see what I can find out?"

"Thank you, but no. I'm quite happy to leave it in the hands of the police."

I looked around and noticed the jack-in-the-box which the colonel had brought with him to my office a while ago.

"Do you have any idea what you'll do with his collection?"

"Nothing concrete. It's early days."

"What about the dog rescue charity? Will you be continuing your father's work with that?"

"Definitely not. I have no interest in it. I think my father gave enough to those dogs. I don't think they can expect anything more from this family. Now, if you'll excuse me. I'm rather busy. I'm sure Mrs Burnbridge will show you out."

***

There was no point in going back to the office because I wouldn't be able to move for mini-Winkys. I was considering taking a trip over to Candlefield when my phone rang; it was Drake.

"Hi, Jill. Are you busy at the moment?"

"I'm just between jobs."

"Are you in Washbridge?"

"Yes."

"Why don't you come around and have a look at my new flat?"

"You're in already?"

"Yes. Your grandmother couldn't do enough for me."

Hmm? What was she up to? She never did anything without a motive.

"What do you say? I could give you the guided tour."

I agreed, but only because I couldn't think of a good reason to say no. I had hoped that Drake's house-hunting would come to nothing. I realise that sounds a little unkind, but the thought of having him living in Washbridge, as well as Jack, was too much to handle.

I parked a couple of streets away, and walked from there to Ever A Wool Moment. Fortunately, I didn't have to go through the shop. Drake had told me that there was a separate entrance to the flat, on the side of the building.

He was waiting for me at the door.

"Come in. I should really have bought some champagne to celebrate, but all I have to offer you is a cup of tea, I'm afraid."

"Tea will be fine, thanks. Milk and one and two thirds teaspoons of sugar, please."

"Sorry, I don't have any biscuits in yet."

"Don't worry; I've just had a muffin."

"I'm really pleased your grandmother offered me this flat," Drake said, as he was making the tea. "I don't imagine I'll spend too much time here, but it'll be handy to have a base in Washbridge. Hopefully you'll come over sometimes."

"Yeah, that would be nice."

While Drake was pouring the tea, I walked through to

the living room. The television was on, but there was no sound. I had an uneasy feeling about the place. The flat was perfectly nice; it was well decorated and the furniture was in good condition, but there was something which just didn't feel right. I glanced back at the TV screen and saw a familiar face. It was Grandma with a freaky smile on her face.

Drake came into the room and saw me staring at the TV.
"What's wrong?"
"Err—it's—" The TV screen was blank again.
"Are you okay, Jill?"
"Yeah—it's nothing."

Over tea, Drake told me how pleased he was with the flat, and that he intended to bring a few items of furniture over from Candlefield.
"Do you get much noise from the shop below?"
"No, nothing at all. I was a bit concerned because of the tea room. I thought the sound might carry, but I can honestly say I haven't heard a thing."
"That's good." I glanced at the mirror on the wall, but instead of seeing my reflection, I could see Grandma staring back at me.
"Jill? Are you okay?" Drake said.
I continued to stare at the mirror.
"Jill, what's wrong?"
Grandma's face had disappeared, and I was left staring at my own reflection.
"I'm sorry, Drake. I've just remembered. I've got an—err—appointment in five minutes with my—err—bank manager. Sorry. Got to go."
"But, Jill. You haven't finished your tea."

I rushed downstairs and back to my car. So that was what she was up to. She'd offered Drake the flat so she could keep her beady eyes on me. Well, she could think again. That was the last time I was going inside that flat.

Chapter 9

I was pleased to be out of Drake's flat, but I still had the whole day in front of me, and I couldn't go back to the office.

I wasn't comfortable leaving the investigation into the colonel's death in the hands of the police. I knew Maxwell would do his best, but the colonel meant a lot to me, so I felt I owed it to him to at least try to find out what had happened. It would be yet another unpaid job, but I seemed to specialise in those. The colonel's son hadn't been very keen for me to get involved, but I didn't much care about him.

I gave Mrs Burnbridge a call.

"How are things over there?"

"Ben's still here, dear. Looking to see what he can sell. I don't trust him at all."

"I asked if he'd like me to look into his father's death, but he didn't seem very keen."

"He was probably thinking about the cost. He only likes to spend money on himself, that one."

"I feel like I owe it to the colonel to at least try to find out what happened."

"That's very good of you, dear. He always did speak highly of you."

"He did?"

"He said you were a little bit ditzy, but that your heart was in the right place."

Ditzy?

"Can you think of anyone who might have wanted him dead? Did the colonel have any enemies?"

"I've been thinking about that a lot. There were a couple

of people he didn't get along with, but I can't think of anyone who would have wanted him dead."

"Who didn't he get along with?"

"There's Simon Sergeant; a sergeant who served under the colonel."

"Simon Sergeant? So, he's Sergeant Sergeant?"

"Yes, that's right. The colonel often used to laugh about that."

"And why exactly didn't they get on?"

"I don't know the full story, but from what I could make out, the colonel discovered the sergeant had been stealing and selling weapons."

"To the enemy?"

"Nothing like that. To small-time criminals I think. There was no espionage involved. It was more financially motivated. The colonel reported him, but the army didn't want it to be made public, so he was never actually put on trial. He was thrown out, and lost his pension, I believe."

"That certainly sounds like a reason for him to dislike the colonel. Who was the other person you thought of?"

"A man named Rupert Hare. He runs a shooting range on the neighbouring property. He started up a few years ago. The colonel wasn't very happy about it at the time, but he agreed not to raise an objection, provided that the shooting didn't carry on after eight pm."

"Was there some sort of falling out?"

"Everything was okay for about six months, but then the range started to stay open later and later. Sometimes as late as eleven o'clock. The noise was quite loud and it really used to annoy the colonel. He went round there to have it out with Rupert Hare a few times, and I believe the colonel threatened him with court action. I think it almost came to blows on a couple of occasions. There was certainly no love lost between them."

***

This was ridiculous. I'd spent all day in different coffee shops, and all because my stupid cat was using my office as a toy factory. Enough was enough. It was almost the end of the day, and I wanted to make sure that Winky had started to move out. If not, there'd be trouble. I'd show him who was boss!

I was halfway up the stairs when I heard footsteps behind me. It was Gordon Armitage who wanted to kick me out of my office so his law firm could move in.

"Jill, I am so very pleased to see you." He smiled.

Armitage hated me, so if he was smiling, he had to be up to something.

"Hello, Gordon."

"It seems that we will be taking over your office after all."

"What makes you think that?"

"Your landlord is on his way over to evict you."

"Why have you called Zac again?" Armitage had tried to get me thrown out before, but had failed miserably.

"I've asked him to come over because I thought he should know that your office is overrun with cats."

"What do you mean, *overrun with cats*?"

"Don't try and come the innocent. I was in the office next door earlier today and I could hear the meowing. There must have been half a dozen of them going at it. What are you doing in there? Running some sort of cattery?"

"I don't have any animals in there, Gordon. I've told you before."

"Get ready to kiss goodbye to your office."

I was tempted to throw him down the stairs, but I didn't want to end up behind bars.

"Ah, Zac," Gordon shouted, as our landlord appeared on the stairs below us. "You're just in time. I was just telling Jill you were coming over."

"Hello, Jill." Zac gave me an exasperated look.

"Hi, Zac."

This time, I was really worried. Even though I'd told Winky I wanted his workers out of the office by the end of the day, I wasn't confident that he would have done it. I'd managed to hide Winky from Zac and Armitage once before, but I was never going to be able to hide six cats.

"Come on, Zac," Armitage said. "Let's get this sorted out once and for all. Then you and I can negotiate a rent for Armitage, Armitage, Armitage and Poole to take over these offices."

"I think you're getting a bit ahead of yourself, Gordon," Zac said, following behind him.

I rushed ahead, trying to think of a way to stop them.

"There's really no need to go in there, gentlemen." I stood in front of the door. "You won't find any cats inside."

"Out of the way, Jill," Gordon said, practically pushing me aside. "Come on, Zac, let's take a look at these cats."

Mrs V was still staring at the corner of the office where the shredder had been. Only at the last moment, did she seem to notice the invasion.

"What's going on, Jill?"

"Nothing to worry about, Mrs V."

Armitage pushed open the door to my office. "There—what did I tell you?" he said. "Look—"

This was it. I was going to lose my precious office. How could I have let this happen? After all the loving care Dad had put into it.

I followed the two of them inside.

"Well, Gordon," Zac said. "I can certainly see a lot of cats. In fact, hundreds of them, but they all seem to be soft toys."

"But—" Armitage was scrambling around desperately trying to find a live cat.

There were boxes full of mini-Winkys everywhere, and a few still scattered across the floor. Luckily for me, there was no sign of Winky's workers, and no sign of him either.

"I can't throw her out of the office for keeping soft toys in here, Gordon."

"But, there were real cats. I heard them meowing."

I picked up one of the toys and squeezed its tummy. Sure enough, it let out a meow.

"Maybe that's what you heard, Gordon?"

He looked at me; his eyes were blazing with fury.

"Well, Jill," Zac said. "Once again, I'm very sorry to have troubled you. Although I must say, I'm rather confused about why you would have so many soft toys in here."

"It's a charity thing. I'm storing them for the local cat rescue. They'll be out of here by tomorrow."

"Ah—I see. Well, we won't detain you any longer. Gordon, I think you and I should have a little chat outside."

"But I heard them!"

"Come on, Gordon. Let's go."

I let out a sigh of relief, and then almost jumped out of my skin as seven or eight of the mini-Winkys shot out of one of the boxes, followed by Winky himself. He was gasping for air.

"I'm glad they didn't stay any longer," he said. "Another few seconds and I would have been a goner."

***

By the time I left the office, most of the boxes of mini-Winkys had been removed. Mrs V looked a little puzzled as she saw them being carried out, but she was so used to the madness that she didn't bother to comment.

When I got back to my block of flats, all I wanted to do was put my feet up and relax. I'd had enough of mini-Winkys and angry neighbours. But it wasn't to be because there, in the corridor, was Mr Ivers. He was arm in arm with a pretty, young witch, who I assumed must be his new girlfriend.

"Hi, Jill. This is Wendy."

"Hello, Jill," she said. "Monty's told me so much about you."

Monty? Montgomery Ivers? Who knew?

"I'm so excited to meet you," she bubbled. "I hope we can be friends."

"Yeah, I'm sure we will." Not a chance.

"Are you interested in the cinema too, Jill?"

"Not so much."

"But didn't you go to the premiere with Monty?"

"I did, yes." Although I'd tried to erase it from my

memory.

"I love movies, and Monty knows so much about them. Almost as much as I do."

Mr Ivers gave me a knowing wink.

"We love discussing movies, and our favourite movie stars. We went to see The Last Stand last week, didn't we, Monty?"

"We did. Carlos Michaels was excellent, wasn't he?"

"First class!"

"Oh drat!" Mr Ivers patted his pocket. "I've left my journal in the car."

"I'll go and get it." Wendy volunteered.

With that, she shot off down the corridor at the speed of light, and then reappeared just as quickly. I gave her a look, but she didn't seem to notice.

"Here you are, Monty." She passed him the journal.

"You were very quick." He gave her a peck on the cheek.

She *was* quick. Much *too* quick. The only way she could have been *that* quick was to have used the 'faster' spell. What was she thinking? Hadn't the girls at Love Spell explained that she had to hide her magic powers from her human dates? She was blatantly using magic in public.

"Jill, you really must come over to my flat some time," Mr Ivers said. "And let Wendy make us all a meal. She's an excellent cook."

"Oh, Monty, you're so kind." Wendy giggled.

"Not at all. It's true. The meals she makes are wonderful. And she's so incredibly fast! I've never known anyone who could make a meal so quickly. She walks into the kitchen, and within seconds, she's produced a masterpiece."

"Monty! You're embarrassing me now."

She should have been embarrassed. There was only one way she could prepare meals at that speed, and that was by using magic. She and I were going to have to have a little chat.

Chapter 10

Jack Maxwell had agreed to speak with me at the police station. He knew I'd been close to the colonel, so he'd graciously granted me ten minutes of his time.

"In all honesty, there isn't a lot I can tell you at the moment, Jill. You probably know as much as I do."

I usually did.

"The colonel died from the wound inflicted by the bolt that pierced his heart. But, as yet, there's no trace of the murder weapon. As far as we can establish, he was in the room by himself, and the door appears to have been locked from the inside. Your brother-in-law was the first on the scene. His fingerprints are all over the bolt."

"But that doesn't mean anything, does it? It was just a natural reaction. When he saw the colonel lying on the floor, he tried to help him."

"Probably."

"What do you mean 'probably'? What else could it have been? Anyone would have done the same."

"He's also the only other person with a key to that room."

"What about the key which the colonel lost? Someone might have stolen it."

"As I said, it's early days. We don't have much to go on at the moment."

"You must have *some* leads? There must be *something* you can tell me?"

"Not really. I'm only seeing you out of courtesy—because we're friends."

Hmm? So that's what we were? Friends? Well, at least I knew where I stood.

"So there's nothing else you can tell me?"
"There's nothing else to tell. Look, Jill, I have to get on."
"Okay. Thanks anyway."
He hesitated. "Are you still on for the policemen's ball? It isn't long now."
"Err—yeah—I'm looking forward to it."
Oh bum! I'd forgotten all about that.

***

I was quite disappointed to find that Simon Sergeant didn't refer to himself as Sergeant Sergeant. He simply called himself Simon, which I considered a missed opportunity. When I'd phoned, he'd agreed to spare me a few minutes, but he'd sounded less than enthusiastic.

I disliked him on first sight. His hair was very peculiar. On the right side of his head it appeared to be very thick, but on the left side it was very thin. He'd done the classic comb-over, which never worked. There's a golden rule if you have a comb-over: Never be in the same room as an electric fan. As we sat in his lounge, the breeze from the ceiling fan lifted the comb-over, revealing the bald patch beneath. It was like watching a cat-flap opening and closing. It was mesmerising.

"This will have to be quick," he said.

I had to force myself to stop staring at his hair.

"You've probably heard about Colonel Briggs?"

"I have, and I can't say I'm sorry."

"I understand that you served with him in the army?"

"He got me thrown out on some trumped-up charges."

"Trumped-up?"

"Of course they were. He accused me of some pretty

despicable things."

"As I understand it, you were caught stealing weapons and selling them."

"The whole thing was ridiculous. Not an ounce of truth in it. I left the army without a mark against my name."

"Yes, but that's only because the powers that be covered it up."

"You don't know anything about it."

"When was the last time you saw the colonel?"

"I'm not sure."

"Please, it's very important."

"If you must know, I bumped into him in town a couple of weeks ago."

"What happened?"

"I told him what I thought of him."

"What else?"

"Nothing."

"Did you threaten him?"

"Of course not. I wouldn't waste my time on him."

"What do you do for a living now, if you don't mind me asking?"

"What's that got to do with you?"

"Is there a reason you won't tell me?"

"Look, I'd like you to leave, now."

"Just a couple more questions, that's all."

"Out! Get out!"

It was pointless; Sergeant Sergeant had obviously told me everything he intended to, which wasn't very much. I could have stood my ground, but there wouldn't have been much point. He slammed the door shut behind me, and as I walked down the drive, I noticed that there was a parking pass stuck in the front windscreen of his car. The company name on it read: 'Western Security.'

Why did that name ring a bell?

***

When I arrived at Cuppy C, the twins were even more excited than usual.

"What's going on with you two?"

"Look at this," Amber pointed to the noticeboard where there was a flyer advertising the Candlefield Tea Room of the Year competition.

"I take it you'll be entering?"

"Of course. We won't *just* be entering—we're going to *win* it!"

"That cup is as good as ours," Pearl said. "There isn't a tea room in Candlefield which is as good as Cuppy C. We can't fail to win."

"Don't get overconfident," I cautioned. "You have a lot of competition."

"They don't stand a chance," Pearl said.

"What about your friends across the road?"

"Best Cakes? Are you kidding me?" Amber laughed. "They've got no chance."

"Have you seen their cupcakes?" Pearl said.

"And their scones aren't much better." Amber scoffed. "Anyway, that's why we asked you to come over, Jill. We're going to have a staff meeting, and we wanted you to be here for it. We're just about to close the shop for half an hour."

"You can't just shut the shop!"

"This is important," Amber said. "Our reputation is at stake."

"I'm not sure closing the shop in the middle of the afternoon will help with that."

"People will understand when they see that we've won the Best Tea Room competition."

Pearl ushered the remaining customers out of the tea room, and then locked the doors.

I joined the other staff at the tables at the back of the shop. Amber and Pearl remained standing. They were obviously going to lead this important meeting.

"Okay, everyone," Amber said. "You've probably all seen this flyer already." She pointed to the noticeboard. "This is the first year this competition has been held, and we're determined that Cuppy C will take the cup. The purpose of today's meeting is to discuss strategy."

"That's right," Pearl said. "And the first item on the agenda, and perhaps the most important, is Jill."

"Me? Why am I the most important item on the agenda?"

"Because, if we're to stand any chance at all of winning this competition, then it's essential that you are not behind the counter when the judges are here."

"What do you mean?" I protested. "I'm better than I used to be."

"True," Pearl nodded. "But you used to be a disaster. Now you're just okay."

"So what do you want me to do then? Stay at home?"

"Of course not." Amber said. "We'll need everyone here. As far as we know, the judges are coming next weekend, but we don't know exactly when. So between now and then, we have to plan everything down to the last detail. Everyone must know what their job will be."

"And what will *my* job be exactly?" I said. "Hiding in the back, out of the way?"

"You'll have a very important job," Pearl said. "And one that you're well suited to."

I wasn't sure I was going to like this.

"You'll be working under cover." Amber grinned.

"Yeah, you are a P.I. after all," Pearl said.

"What do you mean *under cover*?"

"It's important that we know when the judges arrive." Amber was obviously taking this very seriously. "They'll be incognito, and award marks based on the quality of the food, drink, service, and ambience."

"I still don't know what I'm supposed to be doing."

"It's your job to keep a look out for the judges, and when you spot them, let Amber or me know so that we can make sure we give them excellent service."

"Well, here's a crazy idea," I said. "Why not give everybody excellent service?"

"We do that anyway," Amber said. "But we'll give the judges *excellenter* service."

"Is that a word?"

"Of course. It means better than excellent."

"I have another question."

"Yes, go on."

"How will I know when the judges come in?"

"You'll be able to spot them," Amber said.

"Yeah." Pearl nodded. "It will be easy for you—being a P.I. and all. There'll be two of them, a man and a woman, and they'll stand out from the other customers."

"Stand out how?"

"That's what you have to work out. I thought you were good at working under cover, and *detecting* things."

"Not at detecting judges in a tea room."

"You'll be fine. Just go with your instincts."

"Couldn't I just work behind the counter and make a few coffees?"

"Definitely not. We can't risk that."

"Okay, but if you want me to sit out front, I guess that means I'll have to blend in with the other customers?"

"Yes, of course. That's part of the job."

"In that case, I'll need a constant supply of coffee and muffins. Otherwise, it will look odd, and the judges will guess that I'm not just a regular customer."

"I suppose you're right," Amber said.

I sighed. "It's a tough job, but I suppose someone has to do it."

***

"You're here again," Kathy said, as she opened the door.

"Pardon me for wanting to see my sister."

"I don't know why you don't just move in? Save yourself the rent on your flat."

"I can leave if you like."

"You might as well come in now you're here."

"Where is everybody?"

"Kids are at school, Pete's at the colonel's. I'm off to work soon, so this will have to be quick. What do you want?"

"Who says I want anything? I just came to say hello."

"I know you. What do you want?"

"Well—I did wonder if you might give me some advice?"

"Wow, you really must be desperate if you're coming to me for advice. What's happened now? Which of your many men have you upset?"

"I don't have *many men*, and I haven't upset any of them."

"So, what's the problem?"

"Well, as it happens, I have a dance related issue."

"Dance related? Well, that's different. Dance related, how?"

"I was talking to Jack Maxwell a while back, and he was going on about how he was a brilliant ballroom dancer, and how he'd won lots of medals. You know how men are. Bragging."

"Yeah, I know."

"Well, I kind of suggested that I was good at ballroom dancing."

"You? Dance? What exactly did you say?"

"I mentioned medals."

"You told him you'd won medals for ballroom dancing?"

"Yeah. Something like that."

"You're an idiot. Still, with a bit of luck, the subject may never come up again."

"It already has. I'd no sooner told him that I was some kind of ballroom dancing supremo than the woman who was to have been his partner left him in the lurch. The policemen's ball is in a few days' time, and now he wants *me* to be his partner."

"Oh, dear!" Kathy collapsed into fits of laughter.

"It's not funny."

"Oh yeah, it really is."

"What am I going to do? I've told him I can dance, and

now he's expecting me to be his partner."

"Do you want my honest advice?"

"Yeah."

"Tell him you lied."

"I can't do that."

"What else *can* you do? He's going to know as soon as you get on the dance floor."

"There must be something else I can do. How difficult can it be to learn to dance?"

"For you? Nigh on impossible, I'd imagine. Don't you remember when we were kids. Lottie Baines used to come over, and the three of us used to practise dance routines?"

"Spotty Lottie?"

"See? Do you understand now, why you don't have any friends?"

"I do have friends."

"How many?"

"I have a few."

"How many?"

"More than one."

"Anyway, when Lottie came over, the three of us used to try to copy the dancers on the telly. Do you remember?"

"Vaguely."

"You've probably blocked it from your memory. You were useless. Lottie and I got the moves off straight away. We were really good. We could've entered a talent competition, but you were all hands and feet. You were absolutely—"

"Okay, okay, I get it. I wasn't very good at *that* kind of dancing, but *this* is different. This is ballroom dancing."

"Ballroom dancing is really difficult. It involves precise

moves. If you're dancing in a club, you can just fling your arms and legs around, and no one knows if you go wrong because there aren't any rules. Ballroom dancing has specific steps which you have to follow. You've got no chance."

"There must be something I can do. Isn't there some kind of crash course, like when you learn to drive? That's it! Why didn't I think of that before?"

Chapter 11

I was about to leave Kathy's when I noticed an old copy of The Bugle on the coffee table. The headline caught my attention because it was one I'd seen a few days earlier. Typical of The Bugle it read: *Cowboys*. Now I remembered where I'd heard of Western Security. The article accused them of employing staff with criminal records. The managing director, a Mr William King, was quoted as saying that he deeply regretted the incident and would like to reassure all customers, and the public in general, that they would be double-checking the background of all their existing employees. He was determined to ensure that there would be no repeat of this unfortunate incident.

That must have had Sergeant Sergeant worried. If they carried out their promise to thoroughly double-check the background of all employees, maybe that would involve speaking to the colonel? Could that have been a motive for Sergeant Sergeant to murder him? To prevent him from disclosing information about the gun thefts?

***

When I arrived at the office, the first thing I did was dig out what was left of the Yellow Pages. Sure enough, there under the heading of dancing classes were some which offered 'crash courses'. Fantastic! I'd be up to speed in no time. I called a couple, but they had no classes I could join immediately. Then I tried Ballroom Blitz. The lady who answered said I was in luck because one of their crash courses was due to start in a couple of days. Sweet!

"It costs how much?" I gasped.

"You have to remember that you're getting the equivalent of six normal lessons compacted into one super lesson. Hence the price."

"And how many super lessons will I need?"

"Normally just the two."

"So I have to pay this amount twice?"

"That's right."

"Do you do a discount?"

"For what?"

"For people who don't have any money."

"I'm sorry, madam, there's a huge demand for the crash courses. We can fill them very easily. In fact, there's only one place remaining. Would you like me to book you in or not?"

What choice did I have? I suppose I could have come clean with Jack Maxwell, but I could just imagine how that would have gone:

Hi Jack, you know how I said that I was an expert ballroom dancer? Yeah, well, I lied through my teeth. I can't dance at all. Sorry. Bye.

"Okay, book me on the course. Thank you."

"I don't know why you're wasting your money with that," Winky said, after I'd ended the call.

"I don't have any choice. I have to learn to dance in a few days."

"Why didn't you ask me?"

"Ask you what?"

"To teach you to dance."

"You can't dance."

"Of course I can dance. What would you like to see? The waltz? The foxtrot? The quickstep?"

"I don't believe you."

He jumped off the desk, and grabbed one of the remaining mini-Winkys, which was still lying on the office floor. Then he began to dance around the room. Not that I was an expert, but he did appear to know what he was doing as he transitioned from one step to another with ease.

"I wish you'd told me earlier. The course is non-refundable, so I've got to go through with it now."

"Ah well, your loss." He shrugged. "And my rates would have been very reasonable."

"You would have charged me?"

"Of course I would. You don't think I'd have done it for nothing, do you?"

***

For some reason, I'd assumed the toy dealer's shop would be much like every other toy shop I'd ever seen, but I was wrong. It was on a side street in the middle of the antiques sector of Washbridge. I knew the owner to be a man called Jerry Noble. The sign above the shop read: 'Noble'. That was it. Not 'Noble's Toys' or 'Noble's Antiques'—just 'Noble'. A bell chimed as I opened the door. Inside, it was chock-a-block with all manner of toys including trains, dolls, dolls' houses and lots of jack-in-the-boxes. They looked expensive and not the sort of thing you would give your children to play with.

"Hello?" The voice came from somewhere at the back of the shop. A few moments later a plump, well-dressed man in his late fifties, appeared. "Good day young lady, and how can I help you?"

"Jerry Noble?"

"That's me. Are you looking for anything in particular?"

"My name is Jill Gooder. I'm a private investigator. I'd like to ask you a few questions, if I may."

"What kind of questions?"

"I'd like to talk to you about Colonel Briggs."

"What a tragedy. Such a gentleman. Probably not much I can tell you. I didn't know him all that well."

"I believe you repaired a jack-in-the-box for him recently?"

"That's right. He brought it in a week or two ago."

"I understand that you actually offered to buy it?"

"I did, but the colonel wasn't interested."

"Did it need a lot of work?"

"Not really. Just a new spring. Not a long job for someone who knows what they're doing."

"And that would be you?"

"Precisely. The leading authority around these parts even if I do say so myself."

The man was modest—I'd give him that much. "Is it all right if I take a look around?"

"Help yourself, but please be careful. Some of the pieces are rather fragile, and they're all valuable."

He took a seat at a desk and started shuffling papers around. I think he was keeping one eye on me to make sure I didn't break anything.

I noticed that one corner of the shop was full of jack-in-the-boxes.

"Do you specialise in these?"

"They are a particular interest of mine. I've amassed quite a collection, and I'm considered to be something of an expert in the field."

"Was the one that you repaired for the colonel

valuable?"

"Not exceptionally, but a beautiful piece nonetheless."

I spent another fifteen minutes looking around, then thanked him and left.

***

I'd tried numerous times to contact Rupert Hare, the owner of the shooting range, but every call had gone to voicemail. Even though I'd left several messages, he'd never got back to me. I'd even visited his house, but there'd been no answer. That left me with only one choice. If he wouldn't agree to see me, I'd just have to find my own way inside.

The shooting range was in a large, steel barn, a short distance behind the house. It was probably less than half a mile from the colonel's land, so I could see why noise from the shooting range might carry. It was relatively easy for me to gain access to the grounds as there was surprisingly little security—no magic needed on this occasion. I'd been a little worried there might be guard dogs, but that fear had proved to be groundless.

The barn was a modern, metal structure which appeared to have been custom-made to house the shooting range. The large sign on the front read: "Hare's Shooting Range." The large double doors on the front were locked, so I edged my way around the building, and eventually found a smaller door on one side. It too was locked, but there was a small gap under the door, which I figured I might just be able to squeeze under if I shrank myself. I cast the spell, and focused all my efforts into making myself smaller than I'd ever been before. I was barely the width of a matchstick as I lay down and rolled under the door.

Once inside, I double-checked to make sure there was no one around before reversing the spell. It was an impressive set up. At one end of the barn were the targets. They appeared to be divided into two sections: static targets and moving targets. At the other end of the barn was what appeared to be some sort of snack bar, outside of which were rows of lockers.

There was a small office to one side of the cafe. I tried the door; it wasn't locked. Once inside, I spotted a number of leaflets and posters. From these, I could see that they catered for guns of all types as well as longbows and crossbows. Rupert Hare had just gone up one notch in my 'persons of interest' ratings.

Suddenly, the door to my left opened.

"What do you think you're doing in here?" A tall man with a ginger moustache and hair to match came charging into the office. He quite obviously wasn't pleased to see me there.

"Who are you?" he demanded. "And what are you doing here?" He was carrying a shotgun which was now pointed at me.

I cast the 'illusion' spell, and he immediately dropped the gun like a hot potato. Hardly surprising because from his point of view, it had turned into a snake.

"What the—?" he gasped.

"I'm not sure the police would take kindly to you threatening people with a gun," I said, as I reversed the spell. I figured he wouldn't be in any hurry to pick it up again.

"Get out of here! Now!"

"I have some questions for you, first."

"Why should I talk to you. Who are you anyway?"

"My name's Jill Gooder. I'm a private investigator. I'm investigating the death of Colonel Briggs. I assume you heard about that?"

"Yes. But what does that have to do with me?"

"I understand that you had a few issues with the colonel."

"I certainly did. The stupid old fool was trying to close my business down."

"As I understand it, you needed his permission to open the range in the first place. And that he gave you permission on the understanding you wouldn't stay open after eight pm."

"That stupid old fool fought me every step of the way. If it hadn't been for Ben's intervention, the colonel would never have allowed me to open in the first place."

"His son? You know Ben?"

"He and I went to school together. Great guy. Not like his old man."

"So, let me see if I've got this straight. The colonel was good enough to give you the go ahead, but then you went back on your word not to stay open late?"

"How am I supposed to run this business if I can't operate in the evening? The colonel was making a mountain out of a molehill. You could barely hear the sound of the guns from his land. If I had closed when he wanted me to, it would have cost me a lot of money, and I would probably have gone out of business."

"So you had a grudge against the colonel?"

"Don't put words into my mouth. I didn't like the man, but that doesn't mean I wanted him dead."

"I noticed that you cater for crossbows as well as guns."

"What of it?"

"It was a bolt from a crossbow that killed the colonel."

That seemed to take him by surprise.

"I didn't know that, but as I said, it has nothing to do with me."

"Do you actually keep weapons on the premises?"

"Of course we do. A lot of our clients prefer not to keep their weapons at home. Some of them have children."

"And do you have weapons which you lend out to customers?"

"Yes, of course."

"Do you keep detailed records for all of them?"

"We have to by law."

"How many crossbows do you have?"

He hesitated a moment too long. "Two."

"You don't sound very sure."

"Look. If you must know, the records show we have three, but one went missing a few days ago."

"Have you reported it?"

"Not yet. I thought it would turn up. Sometimes a customer decides to take one of the weapons home. They're supposed to let us know when they do that, but occasionally—you know how it is—it doesn't always work out. But these things usually resolve themselves within the week, so I saw no reason to report it."

"But it hasn't turned up yet?"

"Not yet." He was getting more and more flustered. "I want you to leave now. I've nothing more to say to you."

I did as he asked. I had more than enough to go on.

Chapter 12

I had no sooner left the shooting range than I got a call from the office.

"Jill, can you come back immediately." The line was so bad, it sounded as though Mrs V was being strangled.

"What's wrong?"

"Please come back now. It's urgent!"

"I can hardly hear you, Mrs V. It's a terrible line. You sound muffled. Can you speak up?"

She repeated the same words several times. *Come back now. It's urgent.*

I jumped in the car, put my foot down, and fifteen minutes later, I was there.

"What's wrong, Mrs V?"

"Nothing, dear. Why?"

"Your phone call?"

"What phone call?"

Had the SWS started to affect her short term memory?

"Just now. You rang, and said I had to come back to the office immediately."

"I didn't call you. Do you think you've been overdoing it? You're looking a little tired around the eyes."

"I'm perfectly fine. So you definitely didn't call?"

"No, dear."

Was I starting to crack up?

"It took you long enough," Winky said.

"What do you mean?"

"I called you ages ago."

"It was you? Why did you pretend to be Mrs V?"

"If you'd known it was me, you wouldn't have taken any notice."

"That's not true." It so was.

"I knew if you thought it was the old bag lady, you'd come running."

"What's so urgent, anyway?"

"It's Bella's birthday."

"That's why you had me rush back here? To tell me it's Bella's birthday? Great. Happy birthday, Bella."

"I messed up. I forgot all about it. I didn't send her a card or get her a present."

"Of course you forgot. You're a man. Well, when I say 'man' — you know what I mean."

"If she thinks I've forgotten, she'll probably dump me."

"And you'll deserve it, for the way you two-time her."

"Don't get all moralistic on me. Do you want me to bring up your love life again?"

"No need for that."

"You have to buy some flowers, and take them to her. Tell her I've been ill, so I wasn't able to bring them earlier."

"Where am I going to get flowers around here?"

"The minimarket around the corner sells them."

"I've got better things to do than buy flowers for your girlfriend."

"If you don't, she'll finish with me, and then I'll be one miserable cat. Do you really want to live with me when I'm miserable?"

That would have been purgatory. "All right. I'll do it."

"You know where she lives, don't you? You've been there before."

"Yes. I know where she lives."

"And get some nice ones. Don't spare the expense."

"Have you got any money?"

"I'm a bit short at the moment, but I'll pay you back later."

"I won't hold my breath."

"Thanks, Jill. You're a diamond."

"A mug more like."

I made my way around to the minimarket. They had a surprisingly good selection of flowers, but I had no intention of forking out for the most expensive ones. I'm not completely stupid. Then, I headed for the apartment block where Bella lived.

A man answered the door. "Yes?"

It was only now that I realised the absurdity of my mission.

"Err — I have some flowers."

"So I see."

"They're — err — for your — err — cat."

"Pardon?"

"The flowers are for your cat. Bella, isn't it?"

"Yes. I have a cat called Bella. You've bought her flowers?"

"No. That would be — stupid. No. They're from Winky."

"Who?"

"Winky. That's my cat. He's only got one eye — hence Winky."

"Your cat bought flowers for my cat?"

"Well, technically, no. I bought them, obviously, but — I — err — there you go."

I shoved the flowers into his hand, turned and rushed back to the lift. There was just no good way to explain the crazy.

***

After that episode, I needed to clear my head, so I decided to take a walk around town for a while. I'd only gone a few yards when I literally bumped into Betty Longbottom.

"Betty? Sorry, I didn't see you there."

"You were miles away, Jill."

"I was daydreaming. Aren't you working today?"

"It's my day off. We could look around town together, if you like."

"I'd love to," I lied. "But I have a couple of business things to do. Another time maybe."

"Oh, okay." She looked a little disappointed.

I wasn't in the mood for Betty Longbottom. I needed some time alone.

I wandered from shop to shop, and even tried on a couple of dresses, but I didn't actually buy anything. About an hour later, I'd just walked into Lingard's store when I spotted Betty again in the distance. I was about to turn tail when I saw her pick up a bottle of perfume and drop it into her bag. Bold as you like. What was she up to? I followed her at a distance so she wouldn't see me.

Her next stop was the jewellery counter. She was looking at a display of earrings, and as soon as the assistant's attention was diverted by another customer, Betty slipped a pair into her bag. I couldn't believe my eyes. I followed her into another shop where she did the same thing. This time she stole a small clutch bag. I didn't know what to do. I could hardly confront her in the middle of the shop, so in the end, I made my way home, and waited for her outside my block of flats. As soon as she appeared, I intercepted her.

"Hi again, Jill. Did you get all your work stuff done?"

"Never mind that. What were you up to today, Betty?"

She looked puzzled. "What do you mean?"

"I saw you put things into your bag without paying for them."

She grinned. "Oh that? That's nothing."

"What do you mean nothing? It's stealing. That's what it is."

"Technically, I suppose it is. But I've always done it. Where do you think all of those things came from that you looked at the other day?"

"Do you mean to tell me the perfume that you gave me as a gift had been stolen?"

"Yes, everything in that room is stolen."

"Why do you do it?"

"I don't know; it's something I started doing when I was a kid. It's like a hobby."

"No, it's not a *hobby*! Collecting stamps or coins or even seashells is a hobby. This is a *criminal offence*."

"I think you're overreacting. Although I say it myself, I am pretty good at this. If there's something you'd like, maybe you could let me know, and I could get it for you?"

Unbelievable. I was simply too stunned to continue the conversation.

***

I could hear them as soon as I stepped into the building.

Mr Ivers and his new girlfriend were arguing in the middle of the corridor, and there was no way to avoid them.

"You're wrong, Wendy," Mr Ivers said.

"I don't think so!"

"I think you'll find I'm right."

"I've had enough of this." Wendy cast a spell to freeze Mr Ivers to the spot. I couldn't believe my eyes. Only then did Wendy look around and realise that I was there.

"Hello, Jill." She acted as though nothing had happened.

"What have you done?"

"It's Monty. He's been driving me mad. He thinks he knows everything there is to know about movies. I told him it wasn't Dirk Masters who starred in the sequel to The Longest Walk, but he wouldn't listen."

"So you froze him?"

"You know what he's like. I couldn't shut him up. It was the only way."

"Have you forgotten where you are?"

"What do you mean?" She looked around, a little confused.

"I mean you're not in Candlefield. This is the human world. This is Washbridge."

She shrugged.

"Didn't the girls at Love Spell explain to you how things had to work when you're in a relationship with a human?"

"They might have mentioned something, but I wasn't really listening."

"You can't use magic openly in the human world."

"No one saw me."

"Yes they did—I did!"

"Yeah, but you're a witch."

"I could have been anyone. You didn't know who was nearby."

"I suppose you're right. Sorry."

"When you reverse the spell, Mr Ivers is going to wonder what happened."

"It doesn't matter anyway."

"What do you mean it doesn't matter?"

"I've had enough of him. I love movies, and I could talk about them all day, but only with somebody who's at least a tiny bit interesting. He's such a bore. How do you put up with having him as a neighbour?"

It was a good question, and one I'd asked myself many times.

"I'm not sure I'm cut out to live in the human world. Humans are all so boring. They don't do anything, do they? They just go to work and watch TV. They can't even do magic. I really love magic."

"Maybe finding a human partner wasn't such a good idea."

"I think you're right. I need to find myself a good-looking wizard or vampire, or maybe a werewolf. Do you know of any here in Washbridge?"

"Me? No. I'm the last person to ask. My love life's a disaster."

"Ah, well. Never mind. I guess I'll get back to Candlefield."

"What about Mr Ivers?"

"He can stay like that. It'll wear off in a while."

"But, Wendy—"

"See you around, Jill."

"Wendy—"
"Bye."

With that, she was gone, leaving me with a frozen Mr Ivers. She was right; the spell would eventually wear off, but I couldn't just leave him in the middle of the corridor. He was in the way and besides, what would Luther or Betty think if they saw him standing there like a statue? I'd just have to reverse the spell myself. It was never easy reversing another witch's spell, but I was pretty sure I could do it.

I focused my attention on Mr Ivers, and attempted the reversal. Luckily it worked first time. He came back to life, blinked a few times and then looked around.

"Where's Wendy?"

"She's gone, I'm afraid."

"Gone? Gone where?"

"She said I should tell you that it wasn't working out, and that she was sorry—and that it was her not you." How many times had I heard that one? "But she'll see you around, perhaps." Or perhaps not.

Mr Ivers looked completely devastated.

"I know we'd argued, but I didn't think she would just walk out on me like that."

"She seemed a little impulsive."

"Maybe it's for the best." He sighed. "She was a nice girl, but I'm not sure we were compatible. Not like you and I."

"Sorry?"

"You and I have so much in common. We seemed to hit it off right from the start. Perhaps we could—"

"Sorry, Mr Ivers, I'm seeing someone at the moment.

Look, I have to go. Maybe you should go back to Love Spell. They'll probably find someone else for you."

"I suppose so, but if you ever change your mind, you know where I am."

Never going to happen.

Chapter 13

After much arm-twisting, I'd agreed to work undercover, front-of-house, in Cuppy C. Today was the day that the judges were expected. Before the shop opened, the twins got all the staff together for a last minute pep talk, or as they insisted on calling it: a team brief.

"Listen up, everyone," Amber said. "You all know how important this is to Cuppy C. If we win, it will bring us a lot more trade, and that will be good for all of us."

"Yes," Pearl said. "If we win, you will all get a pay rise."

Amber looked shocked; it was obviously the first she'd heard of this. "What Pearl means is that we'll certainly consider a pay rise."

"Yeah, that's what I meant," Pearl back-pedalled. "Anyway, does everyone know what they're meant to be doing?"

We all nodded.

"Jill, you mustn't come behind the counter this weekend under any circumstances."

"Yes, yes. I get the picture. Jill is useless behind the counter."

"We didn't say you were useless," Amber said.

"Even if we thought it." Pearl laughed.

"Gee, thanks. I'm so glad I came today."

"We're only kidding. You're not that bad; it's just that we can't afford any mistakes today. Any other time it wouldn't matter if you spilled coffee or gave somebody too many shots or—"

"Now you're exaggerating."

"*Your* job is to keep an eye out for the judges. Once you

see them arrive, let Amber or me know where they're sitting. We'll make sure that everyone else knows, and then we'll treat them like royalty. Got it?"

Everyone nodded again. I still didn't think it was a good idea. In my opinion they should have given everyone the same level of service. But what did I know?

The twins had taken Barry to Aunt Lucy's, so as I had a few minutes before we opened, I thought I'd check in on Hamlet.

I found him in his cage, rocking back and forth on his wheel while reading a book.

"Hi, Hamlet."

"Hello Jill, how are you?"

"I'm fine thanks. I just wanted to thank you for being so nice to Barry."

"That's okay. No problem at all."

"He tells me you've been reading bedtime stories to him."

"Yes. The subject matter is woefully boring, but it's a small price to pay for peace and quiet. Otherwise he would spend all night telling me over and over again about the things he likes."

"Let me guess: walking and eating?"

"Yes, you've more or less covered it there. Although recently he has mentioned a lady friend."

"How are things with you? How's the reading club going?"

"Very well, thanks. We've had some lively discussions and debates, but there is one slight problem."

"What's that?"

"It's the old story: access to books. There's no easy way

for me to get to the rodent library because there are a lot of predators around these parts. Cats and the like. I don't want to risk life and limb to get a book."

"Is there anything I can do to help?"

"I don't want to put you to the trouble of going to the library every week. You're a busy person; I'm sure you have better things to do. There is something you could do though."

"What's that?"

"One solution might be to get one of those new-fangled e-readers."

"Surely there's no internet in Candlefield?"

"That's true, but I can download the books from RodentNet."

"What's that?"

"I'm afraid it's rather too complicated for a non-rodent to understand."

"Wouldn't an e-reader be too large to fit into your cage? How would you manage?"

"There's a rodent edition e-reader. I believe they're quite expensive. Maybe you could see what sort of cost is involved, and whether or not it would be practical?"

"I'll look into it."

As the day wore on, I began to warm to my undercover role. I quickly realised that the best way to remain inconspicuous was to ensure that I always had something to eat and drink in front of me. And it didn't cost me a penny. Every time I went back to the counter, Amber and Pearl gave me a look, but I ignored them.

"Another blueberry muffin, please."

"There are no blueberry muffins left," Amber said.

"*Someone* has eaten them all."

"All of them? There were three left last time I looked. I haven't eaten three, have I?"

"No, Jill. The man over there had one. But you've eaten the other two."

"In that case, I'll have a slice of carrot cake. A small one."

"There you go." Pearl banged the plate down on the counter.

Ungrateful, if you ask me. There I was, working my backside off, and that was all the thanks I got.

Just before midday, I noticed a couple come into the tea room. The man was dressed in a smart pinstriped suit; the woman was also wearing a smart business suit. They looked around, and I realised that there were no empty tables. Oh, no! This was a disaster! If the judges couldn't even get seated, what chance did we have of winning? I spotted a young couple at a window seat. They'd been nursing the same milkshakes for the last three quarters of an hour.

"Have you finished with these?" Before they could answer, I'd snatched their glasses away. "Thank you for your custom."

They both mumbled something as I ushered them to the door. Then I caught the eye of the smartly dressed couple.

"There's a table over here."

The man nodded his thanks, and I made my way surreptitiously around the back of the counter.

"Psst! Amber!"

"What is it?"

"The judges are here. They've taken the window table over there. The man at the counter in the suit; he's one of them."

Amber gave me the thumbs up, and then she whispered something to Pearl, who in turn passed it on to the other staff members.

The twins pandered to the judges from the moment they sat down until the moment they left. They were given refills without asking, and were even offered a free cupcake. I still wasn't convinced this was a good idea. I'd overheard one of the other customers say, "How come they get a refill?"

When the judges had left, Amber and Pearl said that I'd done a good job, and that the first prize was in the bag.

Go me!

***

Why on earth had I promised Hamlet that I'd try and get him a rodent edition e-reader. And where was I even meant to find one? I grabbed the Candlefield Pages, with little hope that I'd find anything, but sure enough, there under R for Rodent, was a section for rodent supplies. And the largest advert under that section was a shop called 'Everything Rodent'.

The address was just south of the park where I often took Barry. It was a nice day, so I took a walk over there. The sign outside the shop was purple, and very large. The window was full of everything a rodent could wish for: miniaturised electronics, books, exercise equipment, and furniture. I took a deep breath and went inside. The man who greeted me introduced himself as Bill Ratman.

"Bill? Short for William?" I said.

"No, actually it's short for Ger-bill." He laughed. "Only

kidding. Yes, I'm William, Bill to my friends. How can I help you, today?"

"I've recently bought a hamster for my dog, Barry."

"Good idea. Dogs make very good owners."

"Well, it seems that Hamlet, that's the hamster, is something of a reader."

"Most of them are. A lot of them join book clubs."

"Hamlet's just started his own."

"That doesn't surprise me."

"He's asked me to look into the possibility of getting a rodent edition e-reader."

"We have quite a selection. Over there, on the far wall."

"Is it okay if I take a look?"

"Sure—help yourself."

The shop had an extensive selection of rodent edition TVs, iPods, and all manner of electronics. There were five e-readers in total. They looked just the ticket, but then I spotted the prices. I couldn't believe it. The cheapest one was three times the price of an e-reader in the human world. I'd already spent a small fortune on the hamster; I wasn't going to spend that kind of money on an e-reader.

"Did you see anything you liked?" Bill shouted, as I made my way to the door.

"They're a little too expensive, I'm afraid. I'll leave it for now."

"Okay, well you know where I am."

Sorry, Hamlet, you look like sticking with conventional paperbacks.

***

Back in Washbridge, Winky was at my desk *again*.

"What have I told you about using my computer?"
"Hush woman, I'm busy."
"So am I. I've got cases to solve."
"No you haven't. Look, I need your opinion on something."
"You want *my* opinion? What exactly are you doing?" I tried to look over his shoulder.
"Do you remember I told you that I'd licensed the mini-Winky to a large company?"
"Yes, how's that going?"
"Very well. In fact, so well that they've now decided to sell a range of clothing for the doll, and they've asked me to come up with a few suggestions. So, I'm just playing around with a few ideas, and I wondered what you thought of them."
"Go on, then. Let's have a look."
"The first one is a tennis player's outfit. I think the shorts suit me, don't you?"
He had the photo of the mini-Winky on screen, and he'd somehow managed to superimpose a white tennis outfit onto it.
"Err — it doesn't really flatter your legs, does it?"
"What's wrong with my legs?"
"They're a bit on the fat side."
"I don't have fat legs!" He glanced down at them. "They're in perfect proportion to my body."
"Yeah, but then you've got a fat body as well."
"Cheek! Anyway, what do you think of the outfit?"
"It's okay, but it's not really you, is it?"
"How do you mean?"
"When was the last time you played tennis?"
"I've never played."

"Exactly."

"I think you're missing the point. This is all about merchandising. Take a look at the next one."

"What are you meant to be there exactly?" This time the mini-Winky was wearing a sparkly jacket and sparkly trousers, and was holding a microphone.

"That's me as a pop star, obviously."

"Can you actually sing?"

"Once again, Jill, you're missing the point. Just focus on the outfit."

"The pink jacket does match the eye patch rather nicely."

"That's what I thought."

"I'm not sure about the yellow trousers, though."

"Do you think they should be pink to go with the jacket? Or maybe purple?"

"Purple, yes, that could work."

"Good feedback." He flicked to the next image.

"Where is the mini-Winky?" I stared at the screen.

"It's right there. Are you blind?"

"Oh, sorry. I couldn't see it because of the camouflage."

"You're so funny." He sighed. "Have you ever thought of doing stand-up?"

"I have actually."

"Don't bother."

"So, what exactly is that meant to be? Army?"

"Special Forces, obviously."

"That would explain the gun and the knife. Aren't you a little out of shape to be Special Forces?"

"How many times do I have to tell you? It's all about the merchandising."

"But surely the outfits you wear have to be at least a

little bit credible?"

"What would *you* suggest then?"

"Gangster, maybe. Or ballerina?"

"I should have known better than to expect you to take this seriously."

Chapter 14

Mrs V came into my office and closed the door behind her. She looked rather confused.

"Is something the matter, Mrs V?"

"There's a very strange young man out there."

"Strange how?"

"In the way he's dressed. He appears to be wearing some kind of catsuit—it's rather ill-fitting, if you ask me. His name is Blaze."

"It's okay. I know him."

"And is that really his name?"

"It's more of a nickname, I suppose. But that's what everyone calls him."

"And does he always dress like that?"

"He does actually. Will you show him in?"

"Hi, Jill." Blaze had a huge smile on his face. He was sporting a luminous pink catsuit.

"Does Daze know you're wearing that?"

"No. You won't tell her, will you?"

"Your secret's safe with me."

Daze didn't approve of luminous colours, so Blaze only wore them when she wasn't around.

"What brings you here? Is Daze okay?"

"That's why I've come to see you."

"There's nothing wrong, is there?"

"No, nothing's wrong. At least, she isn't ill or injured. She's just a bit grumpy; a bit down in the dumps."

"Any idea why?"

"I know precisely why. It's ages since she's had a date. Decades, in fact."

"But surely Daze isn't that old?"

"Much older than she looks, but then we're sup-sups, remember. We age like witches do. She'd never admit it, but I think she gets quite lonely at times."

Curiously, I'd never pictured Daze in a relationship, but I suppose everybody needs someone.

"Why did you come to see me?"

"I'm here for some advice. I'd really value your opinion."

"On what?"

"There's another Rogue Retriever, who I know Daze fancies, but she's way too shy to do anything about it."

"Daze? Shy? Are we talking about the same person?"

"I know she comes across as confident and even brash, but that's only in her professional life. When it comes to relationships, she's really very shy. There's no way she would ever make the first move."

"That surprises me. But I still don't know what you want me to do."

"I've got a feeling that Haze likes her too, so I was just wondering if I should play Cupid?"

"Hold on a minute! Haze? Is that really his name?"

"Yeah. Why?"

"Daze and Haze?" I laughed.

"Huh?" Blaze looked blank.

"Never mind."

"So do you think I should play matchmaker?"

"You're on very dangerous ground. I mean, what if you're wrong? What if he doesn't like her? Guess who'll get the blame if it all goes pear-shaped?"

"You're probably right, but you know what? I'm going to go for it, anyway."

"Are you sure about this?"

"Yeah, I'm going to do it right now."

"Okay, good luck. Don't forget to change your catsuit before Daze sees you."

"It's okay. I've got a spare one in my bag. Catch you later."

***

Jack Maxwell had called to check that I was still okay to be his dance partner at the policemen's ball. If I'd had an ounce of sense, I would have come clean and told him I didn't know the first thing about ballroom dancing. But as you have probably worked out by now—I don't. I *did* however, use the situation to my advantage. I said that as I was doing him a favour, he should spare me a few minutes to discuss the colonel's murder.

He wasn't very enthusiastic, but agreed to give me ten minutes, so I shot over to the police station, and we met in our usual interview room.

"Have you interviewed Sergeant?" I said.

"Sergeant Sergeant? Yes, one of my people has already spoken to him."

"Did you know that he works for Western Security?"

"What does that have to do with anything?"

"The Bugle ran an article on them—they've been employing ex-cons. The managing director is on record as saying that they are going to double-check the backgrounds of all current employees."

"I'm still not seeing the relevance."

"Sergeant must have been worried that his employer would speak to the colonel, and find out about his dodgy dealing in the army. You know about him stealing arms I assume?"

"As far as I'm aware, he doesn't have a criminal record."

"Only because the army kept a lid on it. Sergeant obviously had a motive to keep the colonel quiet."

"I'll have someone take a look at it."

"When?"

"As soon as I can. We have several other lines of enquiry, you know."

"What about Hare?"

"What about him?"

"Did you know one of his crossbows is missing?"

"Yes, we're aware of that."

"Don't you think that's rather a coincidence?"

"Maybe, maybe not. Like I said, we're following a number of leads. You have to let us do our job."

Typical police. Everything moved at a glacial pace.

The rest of the meeting was pretty much the same. When we'd finished, and I was about to leave, he said,

"I'm really looking forward to the policemen's ball."

"Me too. Can't wait."

***

I'd no sooner got back to my desk than Grandma appeared in the doorway.

"Hello young lady. I can see you're not busy *as usual*."

"I'm actually working on—"

"Save your flannel for someone who cares. The reason I'm here is that I've decided to let you help me with a makeover."

I laughed, but immediately realised that was the wrong response.

"Why do you need a makeover?" Apart from the obvious.

"For the Glamorous Grandmother competition, of course, why else? And I have to admit, you do have a certain style."

"Thank you." Was that actually a compliment?

"Don't let it go to your head. I mean, the only other people I can turn to are Lucy and the twins. And let's be honest, none of them has any fashion sense whatsoever. So that just leaves me with you."

"When did you want to do this?"

"Right now. I thought we could start by picking a dress." She made for the door. "Come on. What are you waiting for? Let's get going."

As we left, I noticed that Winky was hiding under the sofa; it was his go-to place whenever Grandma was around.

Our first stop was Lulu's, which was a small, but expensive boutique not far from my office.

"What size are you, Grandma?

"Ten."

I nearly choked. "Pardon?"

"Size ten."

She was no more a size ten than I was Santa Claus. She was a size fourteen if she was an inch.

"Are you sure?"

"Can't you tell?"

I looked her up and down. "Yeah—I guess."

She picked out a couple of dresses. One was bright

yellow, the other a strange shade of green.

"Are you sure about the colour? Wouldn't you like something a little more—err—conservative?"

"I'm beginning to think I made a mistake asking you to help me. I thought you understood fashion."

"Sorry."

"Hey, Jill!" A familiar voice called my name.

Daze rushed over so quickly that I thought she was going to knock me over.

"Steady on, Daze. Are you okay?"

"I'm great, thanks."

She really did look great; she was absolutely glowing. I'd never seen her look so happy, or have such a bounce in her step.

"What's going on?" I asked. "Why are you looking so pleased with life?"

"Can you keep a secret?"

"Me? Of course—what is it?"

"You mustn't tell anyone, but I've got a date. It's the first one I've had in ages."

"That's fantastic. Who's the lucky man?"

"Haze. He's another Rogue Retriever."

"Daze and Haze—sounds like a match made in heaven."

"Oh yeah. That hadn't occurred to me."

Huh?

"He asked me out, completely out of the blue. I'm still in shock."

"I'm really pleased for you."

"Whatever you do, don't tell Blaze, will you?"

"My lips are sealed."

"Jill!" Grandma yelled across the shop. "Come on, I need to try these on."

"You want me to go in the changing room with you?"

"Yes, I want you to tell me what you think."

Daze gave me a sympathetic smile, and went on her way. It seemed that Blaze had been as good as his word.

I tried my best to avert my eyes as Grandma struggled to get into the first dress. She'd barely got it over her backside when I heard a horrible tearing sound.

"This dress obviously has the wrong size label in it." Grandma threw it to the floor.

While she wasn't watching, I cast the 'take it back' spell, and within moments it was back to its original state. She had the same problem with the second dress, but at least this time she had the good sense not to force it.

"We're not going to get anything from this shop," she said. "They obviously have all of the sizes mixed up. Let's try somewhere else."

Four shops later, Grandma picked out a floral mini-dress. It was hideous.

"What do you think, Jill?"

"Err—I'm not sure it's really you."

She checked the mirror. "Look! It shows off my legs."

That was the problem; it did show off her legs. And trust me, that was not a good thing.

"I'll take this one," she said to the bemused young woman behind the counter.

I managed to catch a word with the assistant as Grandma was leaving the shop. "Excuse me, what size is that dress?"

"Well." She glanced at Grandma. "It's actually a

fourteen, but the lady insists it's a ten, so I guess it's a ten."

Next stop was the shoe shop. I assumed she'd go for some plain, mid heel court shoes, but instead she headed straight for the high heels. The *very* high heels!

"Are you sure you'll be able to walk in those? Remember your bunions."

"I really did overestimate your knowledge of fashion, didn't I? Which pair do you think? The red or the purple?"

"I'm not really sure either of them will go with that dress."

"Red it is, then."

She forced one shoe onto her foot, then the other, and then tried to stand up.

"Here Grandma, take my hand."

"I don't need your help."

Somehow, she managed to get to her feet, and then hobble across the room to the mirror.

"Oh yes. They're just the ticket. I'll take these please, young woman."

I assumed we were done, but I should have known better.

"Now we need to buy make-up," she said.

Grandma made a beeline for the most expensive product line in the shop. There, she tried to catch the eye of the young woman who was standing behind the counter, wearing a white smock—presumably she was about to perform some kind of laboratory experiment.

"Young lady, I need you to make me beautiful."

The expression on the poor woman's face was a picture. The product which would make Grandma beautiful had yet to be invented. Still, I had to give the woman her due, she gave Grandma a full makeover using all manner of creams, lotions and powders. By the time she'd finished, I had to admit it was a vast improvement. Now she was only ugly, as opposed to *really, really* ugly.

***

I felt sure I was missing something in relation to the colonel's murder, and I hoped I might find some inspiration by returning to the scene of the crime. When I arrived at the colonel's house, I parked next to a van with the word 'Noble' on the side.

"Hello again, young lady." Jerry Noble wound down his side-window.

"Mr Noble. Here to buy the jack-in-the-box?"

"I had hoped to, but it's not to be, I'm afraid."

"Ben asking too much for it?"

"It's not the money. The piece has been damaged since I last saw it. The inside of the box has been badly scored, which has effectively rendered it worthless. Shame really, because it was a wonderful piece. Anyway, I must make tracks—I have another appointment in twenty minutes."

Mrs Burnbridge invited me into the kitchen where she gave me tea and a scone.

"Where's Peter?" I asked.

"I don't know, dear. I haven't seen him yet today."

"How have things been?"

"It's been hard. Really hard. I would have preferred to pack my bags and leave, but I thought I owed it to the colonel to keep going until his Will has been read."

"Do you have any knitting projects planned for when you retire?"

"A few. I thought I might visit that new shop in Washbridge. I forget what it's called."

"Do you mean Ever A Wool Moment?"

"Yes, that's the one."

"It's my grandmother's shop."

"Well, well. Someone told me they were selling some strange kind of knitting needles in there."

"That would be the One-Size Needles. It's one of Grandma's inventions. They apparently adjust their size according to the pattern you're using."

"How very clever. What will they think of next?"

"She also has Everlasting Wool."

"What on earth is that?"

"It's a bit complicated, but essentially, you take out a subscription, and the wool never runs out."

"Well I never." She took a sip of her tea. "Ben's never been away from the house." I could sense the disapproval in her voice. "He's always under my feet."

"Has he told you what his plans are?"

"Oh yes. He was only too eager to let me know that he intends to sell the house and contents as soon as he can. In fact, between you and me, he's already started to sell a few things. It's not right. He should have the decency to wait until his father's Will has been read. In fact, that toy dealer was here just now. I think Ben was showing him the jack-in-the-box."

"Is it okay if I take a walk through to the toy room?"

"I don't see why not, dear."

The toy room was much the same as the last time I'd seen it, but today the toys seemed sad somehow. The whole room had a morbid feel about it. On the table in the corner was the jack-in-the-box. I opened the lid, and could immediately see the score marks which Jerry Noble had mentioned.

"Why are you here, again?"

I hadn't heard Ben come into the room.

"I'm trying to find anything which might lead to your father's murderer."

"Well you won't find anything here, and I've already told you, these matters are best left to the police. Now, if you wouldn't mind leaving."

"Mrs Burnbridge said you came to the house a few days ago. Why come when you knew your father would be away?"

"I've got nothing else to say to you. Now, please leave before I call the police."

It was pointless to argue, so I made my way back to my car.

Why wouldn't Ben tell me about his recent visit to the house? What did he have to hide? According to Mrs Burnbridge he'd stayed over because he was visiting a friend. A man like Ben probably didn't have too many of those.

But I knew of one, not a million miles away.

Chapter 15

Rupert Hare wasn't very pleased to see me, but at least he didn't point a shotgun at me this time.

"What do you want? I'm busy."

"One question, and then I'll leave you alone."

"Hurry up then."

"You mentioned that you know the colonel's son."

"Ben, yeah. I went to school with him. What of it?"

"When was the last time you saw him?"

"He came to visit me a few days ago."

"Had you been expecting him?"

"No. He turned up out of the blue, but that wasn't unusual. We had a laugh, and to be honest, I probably drank too much. The next morning, I woke up with one heck of a hangover."

"What about Ben? Did he drink too much as well?"

"Yeah, but he could always drink me under the table."

"How long did he stay?"

"He was gone by the time I got up the next morning. I assumed he'd gone back home or to the colonel's house."

"Tell me, Mr Hare, when did your crossbow go missing?"

"I'm not sure—a few days ago, maybe."

"Was it before or after Ben came to visit you?"

"It must have been about the same time, I suppose." His expression changed. "Hold on! Ben wouldn't have taken it, if that's what you're thinking. He'd never steal from me. You're barking up the wrong tree."

Maybe, maybe not.

***

The door to my office flew open, and Kathy came charging in. I could tell immediately that something was wrong. Her eyes were red from crying, and she could barely speak.

"What's the matter? Come and sit down."

I managed to guide her over to the sofa. She was in a terrible state — shaking and crying. I was struggling to get any sense out of her at all.

"What is it?"

"Pete, it's Pete—"

"What's happened to him? Is he all right? Is he hurt?"

"No." She shook her head.

"What then? What's the matter?"

She took a deep breath. "He's been arrested. They're going to charge him with the colonel's murder."

"What? Why would they do that?"

"I have no idea. I just got a phone call. They've taken him to the police station. You've got to help him, Jill. Please help him."

"Don't worry, I'll sort it out. It's obviously a mistake. Sit tight. I'll make a phone call."

I went out to see Mrs V. "Can you make a cup of strong, sweet tea for Kathy?"

"Is she okay?"

"She will be. She's just had a nasty shock."

While Mrs V made the tea, I stayed in the outer office and made a call. Much to my surprise, I actually got through to Jack Maxwell first time.

"Jack, what's going on? Why have you arrested Peter?"

"I'm sorry, Jill. I couldn't tell you earlier in case you warned him."

"Warned him of what? That the Washbridge police are useless? What were you thinking? You know Peter could never do something like this."

"All the evidence points to him."

"What evidence?"

"His fingerprints are on the bolt."

"He explained that!"

"He has the only key."

"What about the one that went missing?"

"And we've just found the crossbow in his shed."

That took the wind out of my sails for a moment, but I quickly recovered.

"The colonel's son must have planted it there. He was up here a few days before the colonel was murdered. It turns out he's quite friendly with Rupert Hare who owns the shooting range on the next property. A crossbow went missing from the range around the same time as Ben was here."

"Did Hare actually say that Ben took it?"

"No. In fact, he's adamant that he didn't."

"What proof do you have that he did, then?"

"None as yet. I've only just found out about it myself, but surely it must cast doubt on Peter's guilt. My guess is that Ben took the crossbow, killed his father and then planted it in Peter's shed. He must have known that the police would uncover it sooner or later, and put two and two together and get five."

"Ever the diplomat."

"Sorry. But now you know Ben stole the crossbow, surely you have to take another look at him?"

"And we will."

"So you'll release Peter?"

"I can't make any promises."

"That's ridiculous! You have to—"

"Sorry, Jill. I have to go. I'll keep you posted."

Mrs V's cup of tea had calmed Kathy down a little, so I brought her up-to-date.

"Pete didn't do it!" she said, wiping away a tear.

"Of course he didn't. The police will work that out—eventually."

"How long is eventually? Will they keep him overnight?"

"I hope not. Look, you'd better get back home to take care of the kids. I'll call you as soon as I know anything."

"You have to get him out, Jill."

"I will. I promise."

***

An hour after Kathy had left, I was still trying to figure out what on earth I should do when my phone rang. It was Jack Maxwell again.

"I've got good news and bad news," he said, cryptically.

"Go on."

"The good news is we've released Peter."

I sighed with relief. "What's the bad news?"

"The bad news is we won't be arresting Ben."

"Why not? He took the crossbow. You know he must have planted it in the shed."

"We're pretty sure you're right about that, and we will file charges eventually. Probably theft."

"But surely you should be charging him with the murder of his father?"

"We can't."

"Why not?"

"Because the bolt that killed the colonel wasn't fired from that crossbow."

"What?"

"The forensics show it would have been impossible."

"So what did fire it?"

"We have no idea, and until we do, this enquiry is going nowhere fast."

By the time I got back to my flat, I was utterly confused. I'd been so sure that we had Ben banged to rights. He'd obviously planted the crossbow in the shed, so how could that not be the murder weapon? It didn't make any sense.

I was peckish, so I shoved a couple of slices of bread into the toaster. I was still deep in thought when suddenly the toast shot across the worktop.

Eureka!

***

I was sure I was onto something in the hunt for the colonel's murderer, but it would have to wait because I'd promised to attend the Tea Room of the Year Awards which were to be held in the Crown Hotel.

Everyone was dressed to the nines: Aunt Lucy, Lester, the twins and their fiancés, Alan and William. Even Grandma had made the effort.

Everybody was in good spirits, and the twins were particularly excited. They were confident that they were going to win, and rightly so. After all, their tea room was one of the best, if not *the* best, in Candlefield, and certainly their cupcakes were second to none.

The hotel itself was something of a let-down. It was in dire need of a lick of paint, but at least the room where the ceremony was to be held had been decked out nicely. We were seated at a table very close to the front.

"Not far for us to walk to get our award," Amber said.

"We'll go up together." Pearl could barely contain her excitement.

Alan and William were chatting to each other. They were clearly more interested in discussing BoundBall than they were in the tea room awards.

"The service isn't very good in here," Grandma complained, holding up an empty glass, and trying to catch the attention of one of the waitresses.

"Mother, you've only just sat down, and that's your second drink." Aunt Lucy tutted.

"I'm thirsty. What's wrong with that?"

"We'll be here for three hours. You need to pace yourself."

"I don't need a lecture from you on how much to drink, Lucy. Besides, there's one important fact you've overlooked."

"What's that?"

"The drinks are free."

Aunt Lucy sighed. Arguing with Grandma was pointless. Hopefully she wouldn't drink too much. I didn't fancy the idea of having to carry her home.

For the first part of the evening, we were entertained by a tribute band, who seemed to me to be out of tune, but the twins obviously enjoyed them. After the band had finished their set, a comedian took to the stage. He was about as funny as Mr Ivers was interesting. But again, the twins and even Aunt Lucy and Grandma seemed to enjoy his act, so maybe I wasn't yet attuned to the sup sense of humour.

Finally, we came to the main event of the evening. The compere walked to the front of the stage, and looked out on the crowd.

"Ladies and Gentlemen. This is the moment you've all been waiting for. The inaugural Candlefield Tea Room of the Year Awards."

"It's exciting, isn't it Jill?" Amber said.

"Yeah, very." Yawn.

"We've got this in the bag," Pearl said.

"It gives me great pleasure to announce the winners." Drum roll. "In third place, a newcomer to the tea room scene, but with an excellent score from the judges. Please, give it up for Best Cakes!"

Miles Best and Mindy Lowe made their way onto the stage to collect their trophy. The twins clapped, but I could see that their hearts weren't in it.

"And in second place, one of Candlefield's oldest and best established tea rooms, Cute Cakes!"

Once again, the room was filled with applause, and from somewhere at the back, two elderly witches made their way slowly to the stage to collect their award. The twins again applauded; more genuinely this time, I felt.

"This is it!" Amber said. "Are you ready Pearl?"

"Yeah, I'm ready."

The two of them were already on their feet by the time the compere made his final announcement.

"And the winner of this year's Tea Room of the Year competition is—" Another, even longer drum roll. "Whiz Cakes!"

The twins had actually begun to walk towards the stage, and had to do a quick U-turn back to their seats.

"Whiz Cakes?" Amber said.

"Whiz Cakes?" Pearl repeated.

They both looked at me. I shrugged. "Never mind. Maybe next year."

"What went wrong?" Amber sounded despondent.

"What happened, Jill?" Pearl glared at me.

"Beats me. The judges seemed perfectly happy as far as I could tell."

"And now, ladies and gentlemen," the compere continued. "I would like you to welcome on stage our esteemed judges who visited each of the tea rooms in this year's competition. Please welcome, Paul Andrews and Andrea Davis, your judges."

The man and woman who walked on stage were not the smartly dressed couple who I'd assumed were the judges, but there *was* something familiar about them. Where did I know them from? Then, I remembered. Oh no! It was the young man and woman I'd hurried out of the shop to make way for the couple I'd *thought* were the judges. I'd kicked the judges out of Cuppy C. If the twins realised, I was a dead woman.

"They're not the couple you told us were the judges," Pearl said, accusingly.

"How did you miss the real judges, Jill?" It was Amber's turn to glare at me.

"I didn't. Those two never came into the shop," I lied. "I would have remembered them."

"Are you sure you weren't asleep at the wheel?" Amber

pressed.

"Positive. The whole competition must have been rigged." I was clutching at my last straw.

The twins thought about it for a minute, and then both nodded.

"You're right," Pearl said. "It's a set-up. The other tea rooms must have done this because Cuppy C has been so successful."

"We should lodge a formal complaint." Amber looked most indignant.

"I wouldn't do that," I said.

If they did, the truth would no doubt come out, and I'd be toast.

"You should rise above it. Take the moral high ground. You don't need a silly award to prove Cuppy C is the best tea room in Candlefield."

"You're right, Jill," Pearl said.

"Yeah, we'll take the moral high ground." Amber agreed.

Phew! Another bullet dodged.

***

The next morning, still feeling really guilty about the tea room awards fiasco, I went back to see Jerry Noble.

"Hello, young lady. I see more of you than I do my lady wife. But then we are divorced." He laughed at his own joke.

"I just have one quick question for you, please, Mr Noble. Are you absolutely certain that the jack-in-the-box wasn't damaged like that when the colonel collected it from you?"

"Absolutely. It was in pristine condition when it left these premises."

"Right. Thank you very much." I turned to leave.

"And anyway, it wasn't the colonel who picked it up. It was Ben. He collected it while his father was away."

Chapter 16

It took all my powers of persuasion to get Ben to see me again. He'd only agreed because I'd made up a story about his father asking me to look into the dealings of his off-shore bank. There was of course no such off-shore bank account, but Ben could smell money, and that was enough.

"I don't have time to waste with you." He came storming into the toy room where I'd insisted we meet. "So just hand over all the files you have on my father."

"I don't have any files." I walked across the room, and picked up the recently repaired jack-in-the-box. "And there isn't an off-shore bank account."

"What are you doing with that? Put it down."

"What's wrong, Ben? Not scared of a jack-in-the-box, are you?"

"It belongs to me now. Just put it down!"

"Why are you so keen to sell it, Ben? Why are you so eager to get it out of the house?"

"Put it down!"

I held it, so the lid was facing him. "You and I have something in common."

"I doubt that!" He spat the words.

"It's true. Before I became a private investigator, I did a degree in engineering," I lied.

"So? Why should I care?"

"I was fascinated with the work you'd done on this jack-in-the-box."

"I don't know what you're talking about." It was clear from his expression that he knew *exactly* what I was talking about.

"I decided to try to emulate your work, and I believe I have succeeded. Would you like to see?"

"No!" He began to back away, but I kept pace with him.

"Why don't I just open the lid and show you?"

"No!" He screamed.

"Why did you do it Ben?"

"I don't know what you're talking about."

"It's pointless lying now. Unless you'd like me to open the box?"

"No!"

"Why did you kill your father?"

"He never cared for me. Never once! All he ever cared about were those stupid dogs of his."

"That's still no reason to kill him."

"He was going to leave everything to those dogs. Everything. I'm his son. His flesh and blood. How could he do that?"

"So you decided to take matters into your own hands? You decided to kill him before he could change his Will."

"You can't prove a thing."

"You rigged the jack-in-the-box to fire the bolt, didn't you? You inserted a firing mechanism, so that when your father opened it, it would fire the bolt, and then close the lid, didn't you, Ben?"

"I don't know what you're talking about."

"I think you do. And then after the SOCO had left, you removed the firing mechanism. It was small and easy to secrete, even when the police were around. It would have been much more difficult to walk out with the jack-in-the-box itself. Someone would have asked questions. That's why you brought the toy dealer in, isn't it? If he'd bought it, as you'd hoped, you might have got away with it. But in your rush to remove the firing mechanism, you damaged the box, so Jerry Noble was no longer interested." I pointed the box at him again. The firing mechanism I've fitted works a dream. Would you like to see?"

"No!" He cowered against the wall.

"Time to talk to the police, I think."

"I'll deny everything. It'll be your word against mine." A smile played over his lips. "In fact, you've done me a favour. By fitting the new firing mechanism, you will have obscured all traces of the original."

His smile turned to a grin.

"There's one slight flaw in that theory, Ben."

"Oh? And what's that?"

I slid the catch aside, and the lid flew open. Ben screamed and dived for cover, but then looked up to see the jack had popped up in the box.

"I never actually fitted a firing mechanism, but I did record the last few minutes of our conversation on my phone." I pointed to the shelf where I'd put my smartphone before Ben arrived. "I think the police will find that footage quite interesting."

While he was still stunned, I used the 'tie-up' spell to bind his feet and hands, and then called Jack Maxwell.

***

As soon as I walked into Kathy's house, she gave me a great big hug.

"Get off!" I tried to pull away.

"Thank you so much, I'm so grateful to you."

"It's okay. Just let me go." I wasn't overly keen on being

hugged.

Peter looked pretty shocking, but he still managed a smile.

"How's it going?" I said.

"I'm glad to be a free man again. For a while there, I thought they were actually going to charge me with the colonel's murder."

"So, what happens now?"

"I guess I'm out of work again. I really loved that job, but now I'm back to square one." He shrugged. "I'm sure I'll find something. I've done it before."

"Jill, I've got a surprise for you," Kathy interrupted. A surprise from my sister usually wasn't good news.

"You know I don't like surprises."

"You'll like this one. Trust me." Trust Kathy? Not likely.

She led me into the kitchen. "Close your eyes."

"No. I don't—"

"Just close your eyes. I promise you'll like it."

I did as she said, and waited for her to do something horrible to me. But then, she took my hand, and placed it on something which felt very custard creamy.

"Giant custard creams!"

"It was the least I could do. When I knew Pete was on his way home, I popped out to buy some. I had intended to get the regular size, but I saw these, and thought you deserved them."

"Thank you."

"Auntie Jill, Auntie Jill!" Lizzie came running into the room. "I still haven't spent a day with you at your office."

"I know. I'm sorry, Lizzie. I've been busy trying to get your daddy back home."

"Well, he's home now, so can I come?"

"Yeah, as soon as I can get something sorted out, I'll let your mummy know."

"Will it be soon?"

"Yeah, very soon, I promise."

Just then, Mikey came into the room. He was playing his drum—as per usual.

"I hate that thing," Kathy said. "It drives me mad. That's all he does these days. I bought him a new toy car because I thought that might take his mind off it. But he only played with it for thirty seconds, and then started banging his stupid drum again."

"I've told you before. You should wait until he's asleep, then throw it in the bin."

"Yeah. Great idea, Jill. Because *that* wouldn't cause any problems at all."

"So what *are* you going to do about it then?"

"There's nothing I can do, apart from hoping he gets bored with it, but there's not much sign of that happening."

"I've got a better idea."

"Go on. I'll listen to any suggestions at the moment."

"Coffee Triangle."

"Isn't that the new coffee shop just down the road from 'Ever'? How's that going to help?"

"You know what they do down there, don't you?"

"I know they play instruments. Your grandmother's always complaining about the noise."

"It's a percussion themed coffee shop. Every day, they focus on a different percussion instrument: gongs, triangles, tambourines and so on. They have a drum day."

"Please, don't *ever* take me there on drum day."

"I wasn't thinking of taking *you*, but what if I took

Mikey? The noise in that place on drum day is unbelievable. It's enough to burst your eardrums. It will be so bad that he'll never want to play a drum again."

"Do you really think it will work?"

"It's worth a try. What do you have to lose?"

"Okay then. Go for it."

"I'll take him the next time it's drum day."

***

I hadn't been back at my flat for more than a few minutes when there was a frantic knocking on the door.

"Jill, help! Jill!" I could hear Betty screaming.

What on earth was going on? I opened the door, and she practically fell inside.

"You have to help me, please."

"What is it? Calm down, tell me what's wrong."

"I was in town, shopping. Well, not shopping exactly."

"Please tell me you weren't shoplifting again."

"It was only a handbag."

"It's a crime."

"It was such a lovely blue."

"What happened?"

"Someone saw me and grabbed my arm. I managed to pull away and made a run for it, but I dropped my purse. It has my credit card and driving license in it."

"Oh, Betty."

"The police will be here any minute. They'll arrest me and throw me in prison forever."

"I don't think they'll do that."

"But I'll lose my job if they find out I've been stealing."

"What do you expect me to do?"

"You have to help me, please!"

I could hardly throw poor Betty to the lions even if she had attacked me with a jellyfish. I had to do something.

"If I help you, you must promise that you'll never shoplift again—ever."

"I promise, Jill. I'll never take anything ever again. Don't let them arrest me. I don't want to lose my job. I don't want to go to jail."

"There's something else you have to promise, too."

"Anything. You can have my seashell collection if you want."

"Nothing as drastic as that. I need you to promise that you'll return all the items you have stolen."

"But there's hundreds of them!"

"I know, and you have to return every single one."

"But it will take ages!"

"Do you promise? Or shall I let the police take you?"

"I promise. I'll take it all back. I promise."

"Okay. Go to the main entrance, and wait there until the police arrive."

"But they'll arrest me."

"No they won't. They'll want to see your flat to check for stolen goods."

"But they'll find all that stuff, and then they'll lock me up forever and throw away the key."

"You're going to have to trust me."

"But Jill, I'm scared."

"Betty, do you trust me?"

"I don't have any choice, do I?"

"All right, off you go."

She walked slowly towards the main entrance. I turned and hurried to her flat. There were so many things in the spare bedroom, and no possible way I could hide each one of them individually. There had to be something else I could do.

Think, Jill! Think! You don't have very long.

Then I had a brilliant idea.

The door of the flat opened, and Betty came in followed by two police officers.

"Who are you, madam?" The first officer looked me up and down.

"I'm a friend of Betty's."

"Would you step aside, please? We need to take a look around."

They began to search the flat. They checked the kitchen, the dining room, and then made their way along the corridor and into the first bedroom. But then, where the second bedroom door should have been, there was only a blank wall. Betty stared at it, then stared at me with a puzzled expression. After a while, the police asked me to leave, so I went back to my flat and waited. Half an hour later, there was a knock at the door. It was Betty.

"How did it go?"

"They said because it was my first offence, they would just give me a caution. It won't go on my record, and I won't lose my job. Thank you so much, Jill. If they'd found all those things, they'd have thrown the book at me. How did you do it? The room seemed to disappear."

"You must be imagining things. As far as I could see, they just walked straight past it. They must have decided not to go in the spare bedroom for some reason. You were very lucky."

Betty looked confused. She was probably beginning to doubt her own sanity.

"No, I'm sure the door disappeared."

"Let's go and take a look."

By the time we both got back to her flat, I'd reversed the 'hide' spell. The door was back where it should have been.

"I don't understand it." Betty looked thoroughly confused.

"Like I said, Betty, you were very lucky. But now you have to keep your promise. No more shoplifting."

"Definitely not," she said.

"And you must return everything you stole."

"Of course. Everything. I promise."

Chapter 17

It was quite fitting that it should rain on the day that the colonel's Will was to be read. We'd attended his funeral only a couple of days earlier; it had rained then too. The reading of the Will was to take place at his house. Kathy was there with Peter. The kids were at school. Mrs Burnbridge greeted everyone at the door, and then busied herself serving tea and coffee.

After a few minutes, we were called into the large dining room. The table had been removed and in its place were rows of seats. The solicitor, a tall, balding man with a bit of a squint, took a seat at the front of the room. After the opening formalities, he proceeded to the main section of the Will.

"The house and grounds are to be sold. Eighty percent of the proceeds will go to Washbridge Dog Rescue. The remaining twenty percent is to be split between Mrs Burnbridge, my faithful housekeeper, and Peter Brooks, my gardener, who although he only recently joined me, has become a good friend."

I glanced at Peter; he looked shocked. So did Kathy.

"What will we do with the money?" Kathy said, after the proceedings had drawn to a close.

"I know exactly what I'm going to do with it." Peter sounded so much brighter now. "It seems that whoever I work for, I end up losing my job. I think it's about time I worked for myself. I'm going to start my own landscaping business."

Kathy gave him a hug.

"You know the saddest part of all this?" I said. "Ben killed his father because he was worried the colonel was going to change his Will. In fact, by the time of the murder, the colonel had *already* written Ben out of his Will, and left the majority of his estate to Washbridge Dog Rescue. Even if he'd got away with the murder, Ben still wouldn't have got a penny."

***

"It's her! I'm sure it is!" Amber was adamant.

"Yeah, it's definitely her." Pearl agreed.

"It can't be," I said.

The three of us were staring at a young woman who was sitting alone in Cuppy C. According to the twins, it was Jethro's female apprentice. I wasn't so sure. The woman we'd seen at Aunt Lucy's, had been wearing overalls and no makeup. This young woman was wearing make-up and was smartly dressed. It was hard for me to believe it was the same person who I'd seen working alongside Jethro, but the twins were adamant.

"Go and ask her, Jill."

"Why me?"

"We're busy. We're needed behind the counter. Go on, please, go and speak to her."

"Okay, if I must."

The twins weren't *really* working. They were too busy watching me.

"Excuse me," I said. "Would you mind if I joined you for a moment?"

The young woman shrugged.

"I'm sorry if I've mistaken you for someone else, but do you work for Jethro, the gardener?"

"I used to."

"We saw you the other day. You were at my Aunt Lucy's."

"Oh, yes. I remember. I'm Maureen."

"I'm Jill. Look, I'm not asking this for myself. It's for my cousins over there." I gestured towards the counter.

Maureen looked over at the twins, who suddenly remembered something they had to do with cakes.

"They were just wondering, are you dating Jethro?"

"Oh gosh, no!" She laughed. "Jethro's a great guy, but he's not my type at all."

"Really?" I would have thought he was anyone's type. He was certainly my type, given a chance.

"I'm actually waiting for my boyfriend right now," she said.

"Oh, I'm sorry. I didn't realise."

"And anyway, like I said, I don't actually work for Jethro any more. I quit"

"Why? Was there a problem?"

"Well—yes and no. I mean—it was fine—mostly. I'm interested in gardening, but he wanted me to help him with a calendar he's producing."

"What kind of calendar?"

"You know, those horrible ones. The ones with bare chested men on them. It's not really my thing."

"Jethro is having his own calendar printed? With photos of himself?"

"Yes, that's the general idea."

"And he asked you to help?"

"Yes."

"And you said no?" Was this girl crazy?

"I didn't want anything to do with it. I told him I just wanted to stick to the gardening. Anyway, we had a bit of an argument, and I quit." She glanced over to the door. "Tyrone is here."

I looked around and saw a skinny, spotty young man. He came over and joined Maureen at the table. I thanked her, and made my way back to the counter. The girl was obviously insane. She'd chosen skinny, spotty Tyrone over Jethro. And, what was even worse, she'd turned down the chance to help with his calendar.

I was about to update the twins when it occurred to me that maybe Jethro still needed someone to help him with his calendar? If I remembered correctly, he was due at Aunt Lucy's today. Maybe, just maybe, *I* could help him.

The twins were obviously expecting me to tell them what I'd found out from the young woman.

"Sorry," I said, on my way to the door. "I've just remembered something urgent I have to do. I'll catch up with you two later."

I was almost at Aunt Lucy's when I heard footsteps pounding on the pavement behind me. I turned around, and there were the twins.

"Why are you two following me?"

"Why didn't you tell us?" Amber said.

"Tell you what?" I said, all innocent like.

"You know what," Pearl said. "About Jethro's calendar."

"Oh, that. Yeah, I kind of forgot."

"*Kind of forgot?*" Amber was still trying to catch her breath. "You mean *kind of ran out the shop without telling us.*"

"Yeah, that too. How did you find out?"

"We knew you were up to something," Pearl said. "So

we had a quick word with Maureen ourselves, and she told us why she'd quit. It wasn't difficult to figure out where you were going. We're not going to miss out on this one."

"All right then, come on. We'll all go and see if he needs a hand."

We'd just arrived at Aunt Lucy's front door when it burst open, and Lester came charging out. He was red faced, and had a suitcase in his hand.

"Lester? Are you okay?" I said. But he was already halfway down the street. "What's that all about?"

The twins both shrugged.

Aunt Lucy was in the living room. When she saw us, her face flushed.

"What's going on, Aunt Lucy?"

"I'd rather not say."

"Come on, Mum," Amber said. "We've just seen Lester leaving in a huff. And why has he got a suitcase with him?"

"He's been staying here for a couple of days."

"So where is he going? And why does he look so angry?"

"Back to his own place, I think. He's annoyed with me."

"Why?" Amber pressed.

"I don't know. You know what men are like."

"Come on, Mum," Pearl said. "Something's happened. You may as well tell us because we'll find out sooner or later."

"Okay. I don't know if you know or not, but Jethro is putting together a calendar."

"Is he?" I tried to sound surprised.

"We hadn't heard anything about that," Amber said.

"He asked if he could pose next to the rose bushes, and I said he could. But then, he said he needed someone to spray water on his chest so it would look as though he was sweating. I said I wouldn't mind doing it."

The three of us stared open-mouthed. How come we hadn't been asked to spray water on Jethro's gorgeous six-pack? Life was so unfair.

"So anyway," Aunt Lucy continued. "I didn't like to let the young man down. It's obviously a new source of income for him, so—"

"You did it to help him out?" Amber snorted. "Not because you fancied him then?"

"Of course not. Nothing like that."

"Hmm, likely story."

"So what happened?"

"That's when Lester came back from the shops."

Amber laughed. "Oh dear. Did he catch you spraying water on Jethro's bare chest?"

"Yes, I'm afraid he did."

"I shouldn't worry about it," I said. "Lester will get over it. He knows that you love him."

"I hope you're right." Aunt Lucy sighed.

"That's very sad and all," Pearl said. "But, more importantly, where's Jethro now, and does he need any more water spraying on him?"

***

When I arrived at the dance studio for the first of my ballroom dancing lessons, I thought I recognised the voice of the man taking the class before mine. He had a sort of French accent. Where did I know that voice from? It was only when the class finished, that I got a proper look at him. It was Maurice Montage!

The last time I'd seen him was when he'd come to my office at Winky's request, to offer an interior design service. He'd wanted to 're-imagine the space' as he put it. What on earth was he doing giving dancing lessons?

He caught my eye. "Aren't you the private investigator?"

"That's right. What are you doing here? Have you given up interior design?"

"Not at all. That's still my main business, but dancing is a passion of mine. It's a hobby which provides me with additional income. What brings you here?"

"I've booked the crash course."

"I see. Well I should warn you that it will be very intensive."

"That's okay. I'm sure I'll be able to cope."

"Have you done much dancing before? It's Jill, isn't it?"

"Yes. Err—a little." None really. "But it was a long time ago. I'm sure I'll pick it up. I have a great sense of rhythm, and fantastic coordination."

"That's good. By the way, did you give any more thought to having your office re-imagined?"

"It's not really feasible at the moment. Money's a little tight and business is slow. You know how it is."

"I do indeed."

The crash course was one-to-one. Maurice suggested that we start with a waltz, which was apparently the easiest of the dances to learn.

"Left, right, right—no not like that. Don't put—Ouch! No! Left—follow my—Ouch."

Thirty minutes later, Maurice was hobbling around.

"How did I do?" I asked, more in hope than expectation.

He rubbed his shin. "I thought you said you'd danced before?"

"It was a long time ago."

"It must have been. When exactly do you need to get up to speed for?"

"I've got plenty of time. It's—a few days away."

"Days?"

"Is that a problem?"

"You do realise that you only have one more session with me?"

"Will that be enough?

Chapter 18

The next morning, I'd only just eaten breakfast when there was a knock at the door.

"Kathy? Lizzie?"

"You've forgotten, haven't you, Jill?" Kathy frowned.

"Forgotten? Err—no, I haven't forgotten."

"Okay then, *what* haven't you forgotten?"

"Err—I haven't forgotten—" And then it came back to me. "That Lizzie is coming to work with me today."

"Ten out of ten." Kathy passed me Lizzie's lunchbox. "I know you said you were going to pick her up, but I thought it might be better if I brought her here. Just in case you forgot."

"Look, I've brought some beanies with me," Lizzie said. "Mummy said you wouldn't mind."

She'd got the zebodile and the donguin with her.

"Great. I'll really enjoy looking at those all day long."

"So, you know the plan?" Kathy said.

"The plan?"

"You've forgotten already, haven't you?"

"No. But just remind me anyway."

"Lizzie's going to stay with you this morning, and then I'll pick her up this afternoon when I finish at Ever."

"Okay, yeah, that's the plan. I totally remember."

"Off you go, Lizzie. Mummy's going to work now." She gave Lizzie a big sloppy kiss.

"Bye, Mummy! Wave to the beanies."

Kathy waved to the two Frankensteinesque beanies, and then went on her way.

***

Mrs V's face lit up when she saw my niece.

"Who's this little lady?"

"This is my niece. Lizzie, this is Mrs V."

"That's a funny name." Lizzie laughed.

"Well, Lizzie," Mrs V crouched down to Lizzie's height. "My name is actually Annabel Versailles."

"Bear Size? That's a funny name too."

"It's French."

"Are you French?"

"No."

"Why do you have a French name, then?"

"Just call her Mrs V," I said. "That's what everyone calls her."

"Okay, then. You can call me Lizzie."

"I see you've brought two toys with you. They're very—"

"Ugly?" I suggested.

"I was going to say unusual."

"This is a zebodile," Lizzie said. "And this one is a donguin. I made them. They used to be Auntie Jill's beanies, but she gave them to me."

Not exactly *gave*. I seem to remember they'd been taken by force.

"Mummy and I like to take them apart and create new ones out of them."

"That's nice." Mrs V glanced at me.

"Sisters?" I shrugged. "What you gonna do with them?" I knew that Mrs V would be able to identify with that sentiment.

"So what will you be doing today, Lizzie?"

"I don't know. I've come to work with Auntie Jill

because I want to be a private investigator when I grow up."

"Do you really? And do you know what private investigators do?"

"Not much, according to my mummy. She says Auntie Jill never does any work. That's why I want to be a private investigator. I want to make lots of money, but not have to do any work. Just like Auntie Jill."

I forced a smile, and said through gritted teeth, "I think Mummy was joking when she said that."

"I don't think so. She had a very serious face."

"Oh well. Never mind. Let's go through to my office, you can meet my cat."

"What's his name?"

"Winky."

"That's a funny name too. Is he French?"

As soon as I walked through the door, Winky was on at me.

"Where have you been? I'm starving. I need food and milk. Full cream—obviously. And who is this miniature human?"

"This is Lizzie. You'll just have to wait for your food."

"Auntie Jill, why are you talking to the cat?"

That was a good question.

"Err—I always talk to the cat. I pretend that he can understand me."

"Get me some food." Winky persisted. "I'm starving."

"I think he's hungry. I'll give him some food and milk. You can sit at my desk, and go on my computer, if you like."

I turned to Winky. "You! Be quiet while Lizzie is here."

"What's it worth?"

"The usual."

"Red, not pink?"

"Obviously."

I gave him salmon and milk, and hoped that would keep him quiet for a little while.

"Auntie Jill?"

"Yes, Lizzie?"

"Do you have a gun?"

"No, I don't have a gun."

"Do you catch bank robbers?"

"No, I don't catch bank robbers."

"What do you do?"

"Well—a number of things. I follow people."

"Follow people? Why do you follow people?"

"To see what they're doing—"

"Isn't that very boring?"

"It can be boring, yes."

"Do you get paid lots of money?"

"Not really."

"I don't want to be a private investigator if you don't get paid lots of money."

So fickle.

After a while, Lizzie got bored with the computer, and wandered over to look out of the window.

"What are these flags for, Auntie Jill?"

"They err—I brought them back from the seaside with me. They were in the top of a sandcastle."

"Oh." She started waving them about. "I thought you were using them for semaphore."

"I didn't realise you knew about semaphore."

"We've done it at school. I can send you a message. Look."

"I'm sorry, I can't read semaphore. What did your message say?"

"I said do you have any chocolate?"

"I don't think so. Perhaps I can ask Mrs V to get you some at lunchtime."

"Look, Auntie Jill!"

What now?

"There's a smartphone here. Is it yours?"

"Err—no, it isn't mine."

"Whose is it?"

I glanced at Winky. What was I supposed to say?

"I think it's a client's. They must have left it behind."

Lizzie's fingers sped across the keys with the expertise only the young possess.

"There are cat things on this phone, Auntie Jill."

"Really?" I glanced again at Winky, who was getting angrier by the second.

"Pass it to me, Lizzie. I'll keep it safe until the client comes back to collect it."

"Okay." She gave it to me, and I dropped it into the drawer. Phew! Another minute, and Winky would have been clawing it from her tiny hands.

It turned out to be a very long day. I'd never realised that little children could talk so much or ask so many questions. Memo to self: if you ever have kids, never bring them to work with you.

It was almost time for Kathy to collect Lizzie. I couldn't say I was sorry.

"Look, Auntie Jill! Look what I found."

"Be careful with those, Lizzie. They're very sharp. No don't throw it!"

She launched the dart across the room. Winky jumped off the sofa just in time.

"Whoops! I missed the board." Lizzie laughed.

"Yeah, I don't think you should throw any more of them."

Just then, I heard the door to the outer office open. It was probably Kathy.

"Come on! Your mummy's here." I grabbed Lizzie by the hand, and took her through to the outer office.

There stood Gordon Armitage. "Not satisfied with having a cattery, Jill?" He sneered. "I see you're now running a nursery too."

"Why don't you report me to Zac again?"

"I might."

"I'm sure he'll be happy you dragged him out here again just because my niece has spent the morning with me."

"I'll get you, Gooder. Just see if I don't."

"Talk to the hand."

He knew there was nothing he could do, so he turned tail and stormed off.

"Why was that man's face so red, Auntie Jill?"

***

After Kathy had collected Lizzie, I was enjoying the relative peace and quiet of the office, but then Mrs V spoiled the moment.

"That horrible man is back again."

There were so many. "Which man would that be, Mrs

V?"

"You know, the lawyer man. Very smarmy."

"You mean Mr Devon?"

"That's him. Shall I tell him to go away? Nothing would give me greater pleasure. I've got my knitting needles in case he causes any problems."

"It's okay. Send him in."

When the colonel had been murdered, I'd had to tell Blake that I couldn't take his client's case, and had assumed that it was now dead in the water. Maybe I'd been wrong.

"I won't be giving him a scarf," Mrs V said.

"Fair enough."

"Maybe some socks."

"Good plan."

Blake Devon was indeed smarmy. In fact, he had smarmy written all over his face.

"Hello again, Jill."

"What can I do for you, Blake?"

"I'm here on the same errand as I was the last time we met."

"Really? I assumed you would have found someone else to handle that particular case."

"My client is still quite adamant that he doesn't want to involve any of the larger companies. We were hoping that you'd still be interested."

It was good money. They'd offered me a thousand pounds just to meet with the CEO. I could hardly say no; the rent was due soon. What did I have to lose?

"Sure. Why not? What are the arrangements?"

"As I mentioned before, he'd rather meet with you away from head office. I'll let you have the time and location within the next day or two."

"That's fine. I don't have anything pressing at the moment."

"Great. I'll give you a call."

After he'd left, Winky jumped onto my desk.

"He's untrustworthy," he said.

"What makes you say that?"

"Instinct. I can tell them a mile off. Definitely untrustworthy."

For all his faults, Winky was a good judge of character, and so I didn't take his warning lightly. I'd have to watch Mr Blake Devon.

***

It was my second and final ballroom dancing lesson with Maurice Montage.

"I've been thinking about this, Jill," Maurice said. "Your only hope is to focus on just two dances. Would that work for you?"

"I don't know. I'm not sure what I'll be expected to do in the competition."

"Competition?"

"Didn't I mention that?"

"You most certainly did not. What kind of competition? When is it?"

"I'm going to a policemen's ball tomorrow. There's a dancing competition apparently."

"And you've entered it?"

"Yes, that's why I took the dancing lessons."

"Tell me. Why would you enter a competition when

you can't dance?"

"I'm sort of a last minute substitute. My partner's partner left suddenly, and he asked me to take her place."

"Why you? When you can't dance a step?"

I came clean with Maurice, and explained that I hadn't exactly been truthful with Jack Maxwell, and that I'd somewhat exaggerated my abilities on the dance floor.

"Oh dear." He laughed. "You really are in trouble."

"But surely there's something we can do?"

"I'd assumed you were going to a wedding, or a family function. I didn't realise that you were preparing for a competition."

"Does that make a difference?"

"Oh yes. The standard will be very much higher. I think you're going to struggle."

"But we've still got today."

"Then we'd better make the most of the time we have."

I found the foxtrot practically impossible. What a stupid name for a dance. When did a fox ever trot?

We spent the last half hour practising the quickstep, which was way too fast for me.

"Can't we go slower?" I gasped.

"The clue is in the name; it's a *quick* step."

By the end of the lesson, Maurice was nursing bruised shins again.

"I should really charge you extra for pain and suffering."

"I wasn't that bad, was I?"

"On a scale of one to ten, you were terrible."

"Thanks."

What was I going to do? If I danced like that in the competition, we'd come last for sure, and Jack would know that I'd been lying. But if I didn't turn up, how would I ever be able to look him in the eye again? There had to be something I could do.

And then it came to me.

Chapter 19

I couldn't believe it was actually happening. It was like some kind of weird and crazy dream. Grandma was taking part in the Glamorous Grandmother competition! Was she high or was I? The venue was the Crown Hotel; the same place where the twins had lost so spectacularly in the Tea Room of the Year competition. Something told me that tonight was going to be a similar disappointment. This time though, no one, and I mean no one, expected Grandma to win or even to finish in the top million.

I was pleased to see that Lester and Aunt Lucy were back together. She'd apparently told him that Jethro had asked the twins to help with the calendar shoot, and that she had just been holding the fort until they arrived. Wow! Could that woman lie or what?

I was by myself as usual. I could have invited Drake, but the night was going to be so bad that I didn't really want to inflict it on anyone else. I just wanted it to be over and done with as soon as possible.

After the usual warm-up acts, we came to the main event. The compere announced there were five contestants who had qualified through the preliminary rounds. They had been voted for by the readers of The Candle. Somehow, Grandma was one of the finalists. I could only assume that bribery or magic must have been involved. He explained that he would invite the contestants onto the stage in turn, and conduct a short interview with each of them. Then, the winner would be selected by the audience, using small electronic keypads on which were buttons numbered one to five.

The first witch on stage was Petunia Merryweather. I

had no idea how old she was, but based on what I knew about witches, I put her at about eight hundred. She looked pretty good considering. Yes, she had grey hair. Yes, she had wrinkles. And she certainly wasn't in the prime of her life, but she had an immaculate sense of style. She looked stunning in the black maxi dress which she'd chosen. Her hair was a weird shade of blue, and she'd overdone it a bit on the eye shadow, but even so she looked fantastic for her age.

The interview consisted of the usual mundane questions. Frankly, it took all of my willpower to stay awake. The next three contestants were all of a similar age, and all dressed very stylishly. They all answered the questions confidently; there was very little to choose between them.

I was beginning to get anxious. The four women already on stage had all gone for a classic, understated look. But when I'd taken Grandma shopping, she'd chosen a miniskirt with a low neckline, and high heels which she could barely walk in. It was going to be an absolute train wreck.

"I'll be glad when this is over," I whispered to Aunt Lucy.

"It's okay, dear. Grandma knows what she's doing."

"You didn't see the outfit she chose. It showed way too much leg, and it was cut too low at the front. And the high heels? Everyone will laugh at her."

Aunt Lucy put her hand on mine.

"Jill, you have a lot to learn about Grandma."

Maybe I did, but I still couldn't bear to think about what was about to play out in the next few minutes. The compere called out Grandma's name.

"Our last finalist today is Mirabel Millbright."

The audience clapped. I closed my eyes and waited for the laughter to begin. After a few moments, the whole room fell silent, and I heard her footsteps as she walked onto the stage. Any moment now, someone would crack, and the laughter would start. The embarrassment would be too much to bear.

But then, everyone started to applaud and cheer, so I opened my eyes. Grandma looked sensational. She was wearing a beautiful, full-length sequinned dress. Her hair was immaculate. Her make-up was understated, and made her look—not beautiful—don't be ridiculous—but not as ugly as usual. Somehow, she'd even managed to hide the wart on the end of her nose. All in all, she looked amazing.

I didn't even register her answers to the questions. I was too stunned. After the interview had finished, Grandma joined the other contestants at the back of the stage. The compere then instructed us to pick up our controls, and to press the button corresponding to the contestant we thought should win. Moments later, he said the results were in. The winners were to be announced in reverse order.

"In third place, Petunia Merryweather."

"In second place, Celia Tunstone."

Surely not—she couldn't have.

"And the Glamorous Grandmother of the Year is Mirabel Millbright."

I was dumbstruck. The audience were on their feet clapping and cheering.

"Get up, Jill," Amber said.

I staggered to my feet and began to clap.

After it was all over, Grandma joined us at our table.

"Well done, Mother," Aunt Lucy said.

"Yeah, well done, Grandma." Amber nodded. "You looked spectacular."

"Well done, Grandma." Pearl looked thrilled. "You looked fantastic up there."

"I did, didn't I?" Grandma almost smiled. "Stunning is the word that comes to mind. Talking about stunned, you look rather stunned yourself, Jill."

"I. You. The dress. Shoes," I stuttered.

"You seem to have lost the power of speech, young lady."

"But—the high heels. Mini-skirt."

"You didn't actually think I was going to wear those awful clothes, did you? You're even more gullible than I thought you were."

***

I stayed the night in Candlefield, and was up bright and early the next morning.

"Hurry up," Barry shouted. "I want to go now. Can we go now?"

"Slow down! You're making my head spin."

"I want to go now!"

Usually, the only things Barry was interested in were going for walks, and food, but now, all he could think about was his new girlfriend, Beth the corgi.

Of course, she didn't actually know she was his girlfriend, but in Barry's mind she most definitely was. He was head over heels in love, and it was quite pathetic to see. But, who was I to stand in judgement?

"Okay, Barry, we'll go now."
"Can we go now? Are we going now? Can we go now?"
"Yes, Barry. We're going now."

Barry's would-be girlfriend lived next door to Aunt Lucy. When we arrived, he ran straight upstairs so he could see into the neighbouring garden. He put his front paws on the window sill in the back bedroom, and stared out longingly, hoping to catch a glimpse of Beth.

Aunt Lucy and I settled down in the living room with tea and toast.

"What did you think of the Glamorous Grandmother competition?" she said.

"I still can't believe what I saw."

"You did look rather surprised. Grandma told me what she'd done; how she wound you up with the mini-dress and the high heels."

"She had me fooled. I was convinced she was going to embarrass herself and us."

"You still don't know Grandma very well, do you?"

"I'm not sure I ever will."

"It was good to go to the Crown Hotel, and come away with a prize after the disappointment of the tea room awards." Aunt Lucy took a sip of tea.

"There was actually more to that than you realise."

"Oh?"

"You must promise never to tell the twins."

"I promise. What happened?"

"On the day the judges were due to call, I was put in charge of keeping a lookout for them."

"So the twins told me. They said you were a liability behind the counter."

"We'll skip over that. Anyway, I was sure that I'd spotted the judges. They were wearing suits, and certainly looked the part—very professional. When they arrived, there were no free tables, so I had to act quickly. There was a young couple who'd been nursing milk shakes for about half an hour, so I cleared them out to make way for the judges."

"That makes sense. So what went wrong?"

"The people I thought were the judges actually weren't the judges."

"Oh dear."

"It gets worse."

"How?"

"It turns out the people I kicked off the table, and practically threw out of the shop, were actually the judges."

"Oh dear." Aunt Lucy burst out laughing. "That is rather tragic."

"You must never tell the twins. They'll kill me."

"I won't. But whenever I'm feeling a bit down, I shall remember this. It's bound to cheer me up a treat."

When it was time to go, Barry came rushing downstairs.

"Where's Beth? I can't see Beth. I've been looking for her for ages, but I can't see her. Where's Beth?"

Aunt Lucy frowned, and I could tell something was wrong.

"I'm sorry, Barry," she said. "I should've mentioned it earlier. It turns out that Beth was only visiting our neighbours. I thought she was their new dog, but in fact they were just looking after her for someone."

"Where's Beth? I want to see Beth." Barry obviously

hadn't got the message.

"I'm afraid Beth's gone back home now," Aunt Lucy said.

"Where?"

"She lives on the other side of Candlefield. It's a very long way away."

"When will she be coming back?"

"I don't think she will."

Barry's tail stopped wagging, and he slumped down onto the floor.

"It's okay, Barry," I said. "You'll meet plenty of other lady dogs. You'll soon find a girlfriend."

"No I won't." Barry sighed. "I love Beth, but now she's gone. I'll never have a girlfriend; I'll always be alone."

I knew the feeling.

"I've got some Barkies for you."

"I love Barkies!"

"Come on then. Let's walk back to Cuppy C. You can have some Barkies on the way."

If only Barkies could solve all my problems so easily.

***

The policemen's ball was being held in the Military Rooms, which was close to Washbridge Hospital. Given my cunning plan, their proximity to one another had worked out quite nicely. When I arrived at the ballroom, it was already very busy. I'd arranged to meet Jack inside, and I soon spotted him on the far side of the room.

"What's wrong, Jill?" he said when he saw me hobbling towards him. "What's happened?"

"I'm so sorry, Jack." I pointed to the plaster cast on my foot. "I was so looking forward to this evening, but then this afternoon, when I was crossing the road, a bus ran over my toe."

"That's terrible! Are you okay?"

"Yes. Just a broken big toe. But I feel like I've let you down."

"Don't give it a second thought. It's far more important that you're okay." He glanced down at my foot. "I'm surprised you managed to get here at all. The plaster looks like it's still wet."

"I think the doctor said something about it being slow drying."

I'd used magic to convince a doctor to put a plaster cast on my foot. It had taken longer than I'd expected, so it still hadn't properly set when I arrived at the ballroom.

Jack told the judges that he wouldn't be able to compete because his partner was injured. He and I drank and chatted as we watched the competition.

"I saw in the Bugle that Ben has been charged with the colonel's murder."

"Yes, but it was touch and go for a while."

"How do you mean? He confessed."

"He may have done, but that recording of yours was inadmissible. It looked for a while as though we would have to try and build a case purely on circumstantial evidence, but then we got a breakthrough."

"What was that?"

"We knew from what you had discovered that Ben had managed to sneak the firing mechanism out of the toy room. We just had to find it. After my people had watched hundreds of hours of CCTV coverage, we finally caught a break. A camera picked him up going to the municipal dump on the same day as the colonel was murdered. It took an army of men, but we eventually found the firing mechanism which had Ben's fingerprints and DNA all over it. We also found the key, which the colonel had supposedly lost, in Ben's flat. He wasn't half as clever as he thought he was. He might be a brilliant engineer, but his understanding of modern forensics is sorely lacking. He assumed that by planting the crossbow, he would automatically implicate Peter."

"He did. Enough for you to arrest Peter, anyway."

"That was just a formality. It didn't take us long to clear him once forensics had ruled out the crossbow as the murder weapon. We would have tied it all in with Ben eventually; you just hurried up the process."

"Wow? Are you actually admitting I helped?"

"I wouldn't go that far. I'd still prefer it if you left us to do our job. But I can't deny that by working out that the jack-in-the-box had been used, you did speed things along."

"Do I get a medal?"

He grinned. "Certainly not for ballroom dancing. Not today, anyway. Maybe next time."

"There'll be a next time?"

"Of course. They hold these competitions on a regular basis, so you won't miss out."

"Good to know."

It was turning out to be quite a pleasant evening. Until—

"Jill, Jack. We've been looking for you."

"Kathy? Peter? What are you doing here?"

"Pete has a friend in the force. He managed to get us a couple of tickets. I didn't want to miss my sister, the expert ballroom dancer."

She obviously hadn't noticed the cast on my foot yet.

"We've had to pull out, I'm afraid," Jack said.

"Really? Why?"

"Because of Jill's broken toe."

Kathy glanced down at my foot, and then gave me a look. She knew it was a con. A smirk slowly crossed her lips.

"How horrible. How on earth did you do that, Jill?"

"I was crossing the road and a bus ran over my toe."

"A bus? How unlucky. Are you okay?"

"Yeah. I'm all right now."

"And you were so looking forward to this competition, weren't you?"

"I was—yes."

"She really is quite the expert ballroom dancer, Jack," Kathy said.

"So she told me."

"She's won a ton of medals. In fact, she's still got them, haven't you, Jill?"

"Really?" Jack looked intrigued.

"You must get her to show them to you. She can talk you through how she won each of them."

"I'd like that," Jack said.

"Thanks, Kathy." I glared at her.

"No problem. That's what sisters are for. I hope your toe gets better soon. I've a feeling it will."

Chapter 20

I was intrigued by the industrial espionage case. When I'd first been approached, I hadn't been sure whether I should take it or not. I didn't generally do commercial cases, and I was more accustomed to dealing with individuals than large corporations. It was also unusual to be contacted via a middleman. The whole thing seemed very cloak-and-dagger, but I guessed industrial espionage *was* a bit cloak-and-dagger.

The other thing that had surprised me was that they'd been willing to wait for me after I'd dropped out the first time. I'd assumed that they would hire someone else to take the case. I should have been flattered, I guess.

Blake Devon had explained that the CEO didn't want to meet at their head office because the matter was very delicate, and the person responsible for the industrial espionage was probably based there. Instead, the meeting had been arranged at what was described as one of the company's satellite offices, which was just outside Washbridge city centre. I'd arrived a few minutes early to allow myself time to take a look around, but as it turned out, there wasn't much to see. The building itself was quite anonymous.

I'd been told to report to an office on the top floor where I found a small reception area with a single desk, a sofa, and pretty much nothing else. The young woman behind the desk greeted me with a smile.

"Morning. How can I help you?"

"Morning. I'm Jill Gooder. I'm here to see Mr Truelove."

"Oh yes, he's expecting you. Would you take a seat please? I'll let him know you're here." She pointed to the sofa.

Normally, I would have done some research on James Truelove before the appointment, but with the upset of the colonel's murder, I'd never actually got around to it. I knew absolutely nothing about the man or his company. Not the best way to prepare for a meeting.

The receptionist made a call. "Miss Gooder is in reception. Yes, Sir."

"Mr Truelove is on his way. He'd like you to wait for him in his office. Would you like a cup of tea or coffee?"

"No, I'm okay. Thanks."

I followed her through to the office, which was also fairly spartan. Certainly not the typical office of a CEO of a major corporation.

The receptionist said I should take the seat next to the desk, and reassured me that Mr Truelove wouldn't be very long. Then she left me alone in the room.

While I was waiting, I checked the messages on my phone. There was nothing very exciting; just a reminder from Mrs V to get some milk for Winky. The minutes passed, and I began to grow a little restless. It was already ten minutes past our appointment time.

Not being blessed with patience, I decided to go and check with the receptionist to see if she knew how much longer her boss would be. She was nowhere to be seen. What was going on? Something just didn't feel right. There was no one else on that floor, apart from me. Maybe it was just gut instinct, but something told me I needed to get out of there. And quick.

I hurried back to the lift, and pressed the 'call' button. The numbers illuminated as the lift ascended: third floor, fourth floor, fifth floor, sixth floor, seventh floor. Just as the doors opened, there was an almighty explosion behind me. The blast propelled me forward into the lift. I hit the back wall with a thud, and then everything went black.

***

"No! No! Let me out of here."

I was on a large conveyor belt in some kind of factory. In front of me I could see a mechanical arm picking up custard cream biscuits, and putting them into packets. I was getting closer and closer to it.

"No! I'm not a custard cream. No!"

I was trying to get off the conveyor belt, but my arms and legs just wouldn't respond. Any second now, the mechanical arm would pick me up and put me in a packet of custard creams. "No! No!"

"Her eyes are open," someone said. "Jill, can you hear me?"

The room was white, and so bright it hurt my eyes. There were two figures standing beside me. At least I wasn't inside a packet of custard creams.

"Jill, are you okay?"

"Kathy?" My lips felt as though they were stuck together.

"Oh, thank goodness you're awake."

I was slowly getting my vision back, and I realised I was in a hospital room. Peter was standing next to Kathy.

"What happened?" I croaked.

"There was an explosion." Kathy took my hand.

"You're lucky to be alive," Peter said. "According to the police, if you hadn't been thrown into the lift, and the lift doors hadn't closed when they did, you would have been a goner. The whole of the top floor of the building was destroyed. Some kind of gas explosion, they think."

It was slowly coming back to me: The meeting with the CEO, the receptionist, waiting in the office, no one turning up. And then I'd gone to look for her, but there'd been no one there. I remembered thinking that something wasn't right, so I'd headed to the lift. Lucky for me that I did. If I'd waited in the office another few seconds, I would probably have been killed. That was no gas explosion. Someone had tried to kill me, and I had a pretty good idea who. It must have been TDO. But how was I meant to explain that to Kathy and Peter?

"What were you doing there, Jill?" Kathy said.

"I was on a case. I was supposed to be meeting someone on the top floor."

"Who? The police said that there hasn't been anybody in that building for ages."

"Maybe I got the wrong address. You say the police are treating it as a gas explosion?"

"For now, yes."

TDO was clever, he would have left no trace. I had to talk to Daze about this.

"I have to get out of here." I tried to sit up.

"Oh no you don't." Kathy held me down. "The doctor says you haven't sustained any serious injuries, but you need to stay in hospital overnight because you lost consciousness."

There was no point in arguing with her, and anyway, I did still feel rather groggy. One night in hospital, and a good night's sleep couldn't do any harm. Then I'd be on the trail of TDO. If he thought he could do this, and get away with it, he was mistaken.

I don't remember Kathy and Peter leaving, but the next thing I knew I was alone in the room. The whole experience had knocked me for six. Perhaps it was better just to sleep.

When I woke again, I was aware of people in the room. Had Kathy come back? Had she brought the kids? Or was it the doctor? I opened my eyes, and it took me a moment to focus. There were three figures. It wasn't Kathy, it wasn't Peter, and it certainly wasn't the hospital staff.

"Hello, Jill," Ma Chivers said. "I'm pleased to see that you're all right. We were very worried about you, weren't we?" Alicia was standing beside her, stony-faced. Next to her was Cyril who was on crutches.

"What do you want?" I managed.

"We just popped in to check how you are."

"Get out of here!"

"We brought you some flowers." She pointed to a small bouquet on the table next to the bed.

"Go away! Leave me alone!"

The three of them left the room without another word. I glanced at the flowers and noticed a small card. It read: *Next time you won't be so lucky.*

***

"Miss Gooder, what do you think you're doing?" the nurse said, looking rather concerned.

"I'm discharging myself."

"The doctor said you had to stay in overnight. Please get back into bed."

I was almost dressed. There was no way I was staying

there after the visit from Ma Chivers and her entourage. I was a sitting duck. TDO must have been behind the explosion, and I wasn't going to wait around for him to finish the job.

"Miss Gooder, please."

"Give me the forms and I'll sign them. I'll take full responsibility. I'm leaving now."

Once she realised I wasn't going to change my mind, the nurse provided me with the necessary forms, which I quickly signed. Once outside, I hailed a cab.

"Daze?"

"Jump in, Jill."

Daze never ceased to amaze me. The woman had a different job every time I saw her. Now, she was a taxi driver, apparently.

"Are you okay?" she said, as we drove away from the hospital.

"Yeah, I think so. A bit shaken, that's all."

"You were lucky from what I hear."

"Very lucky. If I hadn't left the office when I did, I'd have been a goner. Do you think it was TDO?"

"More than likely."

"I had some interesting visitors just now."

"Who?"

"Ma Chivers, Alicia and Cyril."

"That's no coincidence."

"I know."

"Look, I know you're not going to like me suggesting this, Jill—" Daze overtook a bus, barely missing a car coming from the other direction.

"Daze, be careful. I don't want to get wiped out in this cab after I've just escaped an explosion."

"Relax, I know what I'm doing."

"Do you have a license?"

"I have a Rogue Retriever license."

"What about a driver's license?"

"I have one back in Candlefield. Just not in the human world."

"Keep your eyes on the road."

"Like I said, you're not going to like this suggestion."

"Go on."

"I think you should move to Candlefield for a while. You'll be safer there. People can keep an eye on you."

"Not happening."

"But, Jill, you can't—"

"Daze, I'm not going to be chased out of my home by this faceless coward."

"I might have guessed I'd be wasting my breath. Anyway, I hear on the grapevine that there's another group of sups who are targeting TDO."

"Who's that?"

"I don't know anything about them. Only their name. Apparently they call themselves The Coven. Maybe we should see if we can join forces?"

"I wouldn't bother."

"You can't go it alone, Jill."

"Trust me, The Coven aren't going to help unless you figure on choreographing TDO to death."

"What are you on about?"

"The Coven came to see me. In fact, they wanted to recruit me to be the 'The'."

By now, Daze looked completely confused, and who could blame her. It took the rest of the journey for me to explain who The Coven were, and why I didn't think

TDO had much to fear from them.

When Daze dropped me off at my flat, I asked how much I owed. I'd expected her to refuse payment, but she actually charged me the full fare. That woman took all of her jobs ultra-seriously.

Once I was back in my flat, I got changed and then stared at my reflection in the mirror.

"Okay, you can't carry on like this. This man wants you dead, and if you don't stop him, that's what's going to happen. So what are you going to do about it?"

Chapter 21

The next morning, I felt remarkably well considering someone had tried to kill me the previous day. If nothing else, the incident had helped to focus my mind. I'd let this carry on for too long. Enough was enough. Game on. We'd see who came out on top.

"Morning, Mrs V. How's things?" I didn't see any reason to mention my close call. There was no point in worrying her.

"There's a lot of noise coming from in there." She gestured to my office.

"What kind of noise?"

"Cat noise. But *more* cat noise than usual. If I didn't know better, I'd think he'd got another cat in there with him."

"Have you been in to have a look?"

"No, I'm keeping my distance. If I go in there, he'll only start meowing at me to be fed. I knew you'd be in soon, so I thought you could see to him."

"What's that you're knitting?"

"It's a scarf-plus."

"A scarf plus what?"

"It's quite an exciting innovation. It's like a normal scarf, but on either end there's a sort of pocket. That way it doubles as mittens."

"Oh, I see. So it's a scarf with mittens on the ends?"

"Exactly."

"And are they popular?"

"Oh yes, dear. Very. Particularly among my older acquaintances. Hands can get very cold when you get older, you know."

"Right. Well, I'd better go and see what Winky's up to."

Mrs V was right. There was more than one cat in my office.

"Bella?"

The feline supermodel nodded regally, but didn't speak. I shot Winky a puzzled look.

"I didn't think you'd be in this early," he said. "We've still got a lot to do."

"A lot of *what* to do?"

"The people who've licensed the mini-Winky soft toy have come up with a brilliant suggestion. They think that it will sell better if there's a 'him' and 'her' version."

"Like Barbie and Ben?"

"You mean Ken."

"Whatever."

"Anyway, I immediately thought of Bella. Who better to be my soft toy partner?"

"Who indeed? So what exactly are you doing today?"

"I have to come up with a design which the company can work from. I'm going to take a few photos of Bella, which I'll send to them. I'm afraid you won't be able to use your computer this morning."

"What if I have work to do?"

"You never have any work to do. When was the last time you had a case?"

"I nearly had one yesterday."

"And what happened to that? Did it blow up in your face?"

So not funny. I slammed the door shut on my way out.

***

I'd been banished from my own office again, and was just wondering what I should do with myself when I got a phone call out of the blue from Aunt Lucy. She sounded rather intense.

"Jill? Can you come to Candlefield straight away?"

"Yeah, sure. What's the problem? Is something wrong?"

"No, just get here as quick as you can, please. Come to my house."

"But Aunt Lucy—"

"Please hurry."

What could have happened? Had TDO struck again? Surely Aunt Lucy would have said if someone was hurt? I magicked myself over to Candlefield, and arrived outside Aunt Lucy's house. As soon as I stepped inside, I heard voices coming from the dining room. The tone was very serious, and there was a lot of shouting. When I pushed open the door, there, around the table, sat Aunt Lucy, my mother, who I thought was on a cruise somewhere, Grandma, Daze, and Mad. What on earth was going on? Something serious must have happened to get this crowd together in the same room. It was like some kind of council of war. Grandma didn't have a lot of time for Daze, and I had absolutely no idea why Mad was there.

"Sit down, Jill," Grandma said.

It wasn't so much a request as an order. I did as I was told.

"What's happened?" I said. "Is everyone okay?"

"Yes, everyone's all right." Grandma nodded. "We heard about what happened to you yesterday."

I glanced accusingly at Daze. She shrugged.

"Don't blame Daisy," Grandma said.

If anyone but Grandma had called Daze, 'Daisy', she would have pulled their head off, and hit them with it.

"TDO is stepping up his game, and we have to do the same. That's why I told everyone to come here today."

I glanced at Mad.

"You know Madeline, don't you?" Grandma said.

"Yeah. We went to school together. I'm just surprised to see her here."

"She's one of very few humans who can travel to Candlefield. Parahumans like Madeline can see and talk to ghosts."

"Yeah, but I still don't understand what this is all about."

"There's been some very disturbing news."

"What news?"

"We have no confirmation yet, but the word is that TDO is about to form an alliance with Destro."

"Destro?" I'd never heard that name before. Was he another evil sup?

"No." Grandma had read my thoughts. "He's not a sup. He's a ghost. Ghost Town has its fair share of power-mad, evil characters just like Candlefield does, but usually there's no interaction between the two places. The sups keep themselves to themselves, and the ghosts do the same. But the word is that Destro, who is looking to expand his power base, and TDO, who is always looking to do the same, are about to form some kind of evil alliance."

"What does that mean for us?"

"We don't know. We don't even know if it's true. But if

it is, then things could become very difficult. And particularly for those who are seen as enemies of TDO."

Everyone looked at me.

"So you think this Destro character could come after me too?" I gulped.

"It's possible," Mad said. "I'm fairly new to this, but all the intel I have confirms that Destro has a long reach into the human world. Naturally, I'll keep my ear to the ground, and pass on any information I have."

"So what can I do?" I said.

"We want you to move to Candlefield until this is resolved," Grandma said.

"Resolved how?"

"By getting rid of TDO, and if necessary, Destro too."

"You've been trying to do that for ages, but no one has succeeded. What makes you think you can do it now?"

"That's not the point. You're in far more danger in Washbridge than you would be here."

"I'm not moving out of Washbridge. I've told you that before."

"You're so stubborn." Grandma thumped the table.

"I wonder where I get it from." I thumped the table right back at her. "I've been saying for ages that we should go after TDO, but whenever I raise the subject, you tell me that it's nothing to do with me, and that I should leave it for others to deal with. But I don't see anyone else doing anything."

Grandma stood up. She was livid. The wart on the end of her nose was glowing red. I thought she was going to turn me into something unspeakable.

"You are the most exasperating person I have ever encountered," she yelled.

"Thanks. I'll take that as a compliment."

***

I felt shell-shocked after the meeting had ended. I didn't want to stick around because I needed time to work things out in my own head. Back at my flat, I hadn't even had time to get changed when I sensed that my mother was in the room.

"Jill? You rushed off before I could speak to you."

"Sorry. I needed to get out of there. Grandma was doing my head in. Besides, I've had a funny couple of days."

"So I hear. Mad contacted me. She told me about the explosion, and that you were okay. I only just made it back in time for the meeting."

"Where's Alberto?"

"He came back with me. What do you make of what's just been said?"

"It's hard for me to take it all in. I mean, I don't know anything about this Destro character. I don't really know much about TDO. Nobody seems to. That's the problem. We don't know who we're dealing with."

"Everyone's focused on it now."

"Yeah, but is anything actually going to happen this time? We have to take the fight to TDO."

"You must promise me you won't do anything stupid."

"I promise."

I hoped she didn't notice my fingers were crossed behind my back.

***

My mother had no sooner disappeared than Hilary at Love Spell rang to tell me she had come up with what she'd described as the ideal man for me. Well, let's face it, it was time I found someone who I could have a serious relationship with, rather than drifting back and forth between Jack and Drake.

Moments later, she emailed over his details. His name was James Keeper, and if his photo was accurate, he was hot with a capital 'H'. He apparently had a very high IQ — just like me. What do you mean? I'll have you know I took a MENSA test. No, I'm not sharing the results — let's just say they were better than I'd expected.

The only thing missing from his profile was what he did for a living. When I called Hilary back, she said it must have somehow been missed. It didn't really matter because everything else about him sounded great. I told her to go ahead and arrange a date, and twenty minutes later she confirmed that she'd set it up for the following night. We were going to meet for drinks. That way, if everything went okay, we could arrange to meet again, but if it was a disaster, I would only have wasted a couple of hours of my time.

Chapter 22

The next morning when I walked into the office, Mrs V didn't even notice me. She was too busy staring at the corner of the room. I followed her gaze, and there in the corner where the shredder had once been, was a life-size cardboard cut-out. Of a shredding machine!

"What's that?"

"I hope you don't mind, dear, I rang the people who make the machines, and asked if they had any old marketing props that they no longer needed. They were kind enough to let me have this."

"But why?"

"You know how it is with an addiction. It's like a smoker who's trying to give up. They have those toy cigarette things that they hold in their hands to help them get over the craving. Since the shredder was taken away, I've been getting withdrawal symptoms. Cold sweats and shakiness. Do you know what I mean?"

"Not really. It was just a shredding machine."

"Maybe to you, dear, but to me it was so much more. I'd grown attached to that machine. The sound. The smell. The look."

Maybe it really was time for Mrs V to retire. Her marble count was diminishing rapidly.

"So, you got yourself a cardboard cut-out?"

"Exactly, dear. Now, whenever I get a craving, I can just glance over into the corner, and see the cardboard shredding machine. That seems to soothe my nerves and keep me going. You won't throw it out, will you?"

It was harmless enough, I supposed. Totally and utterly bonkers, but perfectly harmless.

"If it helps you, Mrs V, then by all means keep it."

"That's very understanding of you, dear."

I was just about to go through to my office when she called me back.

"Jill, I almost forgot to tell you. You'll never guess what happened."

In *my* world, that could be literally anything.

"The Everlasting Wool ran out."

"What? I thought the whole point of Everlasting Wool was that it lasted forever?"

"That's what's supposed to happen, dear. But yesterday afternoon while you were out, I was halfway through a scarf-plus when suddenly I ran out of wool. I couldn't believe it. It'd been so long since I had to get a new ball of wool that it took me a few seconds to realise what had happened."

"So what went wrong?"

"I don't know. I rang the Everlasting Wool helpline."

"There's a helpline?" I shouldn't have been surprised, but I was. "What did they have to say?"

"It was Kathy who answered. Your sister seems to be manning the helpline."

"Really?"

"Yes, she sounded very flustered when I spoke to her. Apparently, it's happened to a few people. She did promise to call me back but, well, I'm still waiting. And I'm having to use conventional wool."

"I'll give her a call to see if I can find out what's happening."

"What?" Kathy almost bit my head off. "I'm busy, Jill. I'm manning the Everlasting Wool helpline, and the phone never stops ringing."

"Actually, that's why I'm calling. Mrs V mentioned she'd called you, but that you haven't got back to her yet."

"I haven't called anyone back. I've logged dozens of complaints, but I have nothing to tell them at the moment. I don't know how Everlasting Wool is meant to work, or why it's stopped working. Only your grandmother knows."

"What does she have to say about it?"

"Nothing yet. I've been trying to track her down all day, but she seems to have disappeared off the face of the planet. She hasn't been in the shop, and she doesn't answer her phone. She's left muggins here to face all the angry customers. Can you get hold of her?"

"I can try."

"Please, Jill. Tell her what's happened. Tell her it's an emergency—an Everlasting Wool emergency. And if she doesn't sort something out soon, I'm going to walk out."

"Okay. I'll see what I can do."

***

It was one thing after another. Surely nothing else could possibly go wrong?

"Winky, what are you doing?"

"What does it look like?"

He appeared to be packing his belongings into a small suitcase: his little flags, his remote control helicopter, and his collection of eye patches.

"Where are you going?"

"I'm leaving."

"What do you mean, you're leaving? You're *my* cat."

"We've been through this already. I'm not your cat. You're *my* human. But now, I've had a better offer, so I'm moving out."

"You can't just leave."

"Watch me."

"Where are you going to live?"

"The people in the flat next door to Bella lost their old cat a while ago, and they happened to mention to Bella's owner that they were looking for a replacement."

"You wouldn't leave me, would you?"

"They've made me a much better offer: salmon four days a week, full cream milk on demand, and all the toys I could want. Plus, my own account on the computer."

"I take it they're not humans?"

"Of course not. It's a wizard and a witch. Both of them are cat lovers."

"Come on, Winky. We've been together for so long. Surely you wouldn't throw it all away. What about me? I'll be all alone."

"Cry me a river. I'm leaving in the morning."

"Well, if that's how you feel, go! See if I care. Good riddance."

***

There was no trace of Grandma. I'd checked with Aunt Lucy and the twins. Nobody had seen or heard from her since the council of war. What was she doing? Did she know there was a problem with Everlasting Wool? Was she hiding deliberately, or was something more sinister afoot?

My phone rang. It was Kathy, and she sounded frantic.

"Have you found your grandmother yet?"

"No, I don't know where she is."

"You've got to find her. The helpline for Everlasting Wool is ringing off the hook. Every time I put the phone down, it rings again! Dozens and dozens of people are complaining that their Everlasting Wool has run out, and I don't know what to tell them!"

"Kathy, calm down!"

"How can I calm down when everybody's screaming at me? I'm expecting them to start coming into the shop any minute now to complain. You need to find your grandmother!"

"Okay. Okay. I'll find her."

"And get back to me as soon as you can. Let me know what's happening."

"I will. I promise."

Only then did it occur to me that in all the time I'd been visiting Candlefield, I'd never once set foot inside Grandma's house, and yet it was the obvious place to look for her. I magicked myself to Aunt Lucy's back garden, and then made my way through to Grandma's. First, I checked the back window, but couldn't see anyone inside. Next, I went around to the front of the house, and knocked on the door. There was no reply, but I was sure I could hear someone inside the house. Was Grandma in there? Maybe she was ill? On an impulse, I tried the door, and to my surprise, it opened.

There was a voice coming from upstairs. It sounded like Grandma. I considered calling out to her, but then thought better of it. Instead, I made my way slowly up the stairs, trying not to make a sound. When I was almost at the top, one of the stairs creaked. I froze for a moment, expecting her to appear on the landing, but there was no sign of her.

She was talking to someone. But who? I followed her voice to a door, which was open just wide enough for me to see inside. Grandma was sitting on a chair, in semi-darkness, with her back to the door. There was no one else in the room as far as I could see. She appeared to be chuntering away to herself.

"Mirabel Millbright, what are you doing?" she said. "You're the most powerful witch in Candlefield. Why can't you sort this out? Come on, woman! Pull yourself together. How do you expect anyone to have any respect for you if you can't control your own magic?"

I'd never heard her speak like this before. She sounded—vulnerable—that was the only word for it. This was not the Grandma I'd come to know; the Grandma who was so sure of herself. It was like watching a different person. It upset me to see her like this.

"Come on, Mirabel," she said, again.

I felt like an intruder, and wanted to leave, but I seemed to be frozen to the spot. I never thought I'd say this, but I actually felt sorry for her.

"Come on, Mirabel!" she shouted. "Enough's enough! Sort this out!"

Suddenly, she went into some kind of trance-like state, and her whole body seemed to be vibrating. Then, just as quickly, she snapped out of it.

"And about time too! Don't ever do that again." She scolded herself.

If she knew I'd seen her, she'd either be devastated, or so angry she'd tear me in two. I crept slowly back downstairs, and left quietly through the front door.

This was a side of Grandma I hadn't known existed.

I magicked myself back to the office, and was still trying to figure out what I had just witnessed when my phone rang. It was Kathy.

"Thank you so much, Jill."

"What's happened?"

"I assumed you must have found your grandmother because the Everlasting Wool is working again now. Everybody's calling to say it's okay."

"Yeah, I found her. She said she'd got it sorted."

"Thanks, Jill. You're a lifesaver."

"No problem."

So that's what Grandma had been doing. The spell, whatever it was, which was behind the Everlasting Wool, had obviously failed for some reason, and she'd struggled to correct it. She wasn't used to failing at anything magic related, so it must have come as something of a shock to her. Even so, she'd dug deep and found the strength from somewhere to overcome the problem. But I could never—ever—let her know that I'd seen her.

This had to be my secret.

***

That night, I didn't sleep well. I kept dreaming about Winky. What was wrong with me? Why was I dreaming about a stupid one eyed cat? What did I care if he left? I should have been glad to get him out of my life. He caused me nothing but grief. And yet, there was something adorable about him when he wore that eye patch.

Still, there were plenty more cats at the re-homing

centre. I would go down there in the morning and choose a sweet, little kitten. One with two eyes, and minus the attitude. Yeah, that's what I'd do. Stuff you Winky!

Chapter 23

The next morning, I rushed out of the flat, jumped in the car and made my way into town at break-neck speed. I couldn't let Winky leave. If I could persuade Bella's neighbours not to take him, then he would have to stay with me.

When I rang the doorbell, a well-dressed woman, probably in her sixties, answered the door.
"Yes, can I help you?"
"I'm here about Winky."
"What is Winky?"
"My cat. His name is Winky; he's got one eye."
"That's all very interesting, but what's it got to do with me?"
"I understand that you've agreed to take him in, and I just wanted to let you know that it won't be necessary. He's going to stay with me."
"Arthur!" she shouted. "Arthur, come here quickly. There's a strange woman at the door."
Only then did it occur to me that the woman in front of me wasn't a witch.
"What's going on here?" Arthur was a big man—six feet three if he was an inch. And most definitely not a wizard. "What do you want?"
"Are you adopting a cat later today?"
"Are you kidding me? I hate cats. Smelly, horrible things—ruin your furniture."
"I must have the wrong flat. I'm sorry to have troubled you."
I got out of there as quick as I could.

It was all a con! Winky must have come up with this charade to get me to agree to his demands. He obviously expected me to arrive at work today, and beg him to stay.

Well, we'll see who ends up begging who.

When I got into my office, the suitcase was still on the sofa. Winky was fast asleep, but when I closed the door behind me, he stirred.

"Still here?" I said.

"I'll be leaving shortly."

"Make sure you take all your rubbish with you."

A look of uncertainty crossed his face, but was gone in an instant. "You'll miss me when I've gone."

"Yeah, whatever." I took out my phone, and made a call. "Hello? Is that Kitty Cat Rehoming Centre? My name is Jill Gooder, I called you last night. Yes, about a kitten."

I glanced at Winky who was now staring at me in disbelief.

"A Persian? That sounds ideal. Can I collect it later this morning?"

Winky jumped onto my desk, and began to wave his paws around frantically.

"Just a moment," I said, into the phone. "What is it, Winky?"

"What do you think you're doing?" He yelled at me.

"Arranging to collect a kitten."

"Why do you want a kitten?"

"Well, now you've decided to leave me—"

"I might stay, if you can see your way clear to meeting my demands."

"No. That wouldn't be fair. I know you have your heart

set on moving closer to Bella."

The expression on his face was a picture.

"What time can I come over there?" I said, into the phone.

Winky snatched it from my hand, and ended the call. "It's okay. I've decided to stay."

"Really? You seemed so set on moving."

"I can't do it to you. It would hurt you too much."

"Are you sure?"

"Yes, I'll stay."

"Okay then."

"Shouldn't you call them back? To tell them you've changed your mind?"

"Who?"

"Kitty Cat Rehoming Centre."

"Oh, them? They don't exist. I just made them up."

"Huh?"

"I'm on to your little scam, buster. I talked to Bella's next door neighbours. They don't know anything about adopting a cat. What do you have to say about that?"

He jumped down off my desk, and began to unpack his case.

This was a red-letter day. It was the first, and probably the only time I'd ever got one over on Winky. And certainly the first time, I'd seen him speechless.

It felt so good!

***

The weather was so beautiful that I decided to have my lunch in Washbridge park. I had hoped I'd get a seat near the lake, but they were all taken, so instead, I sat facing a large grassed area where several people were enjoying the sun.

"Some crazy people in here, aren't there, love?" The woman sitting next to me said.

"Sorry?"

"I said, there are some crazy people in here."

Was she talking about me?

"What do you mean?"

"Look! Can you see that woman over there? She keeps pretending to throw something. Then she waits a minute and does it again."

Sure enough, the young woman did appear to be doing just that. Every now and then she'd bend down as though she was picking something up, then pull her arm back, and perform a kind of throwing action. Except that she didn't actually have a ball or anything to throw. And there was no one to throw it to.

"I see what you mean."

Just as I said that, the 'crazy woman' turned to face me, and I realised it was Mad. I hadn't recognised her at first because I still wasn't used to seeing her dressed as a librarian. She had her hair in a bun, and was wearing what appeared to be a grey knitted suit. I thought I'd better go and check that she was okay.

"Mad!"

She turned around. "Jill! Hi. I didn't realise you came into the park at lunch time."

"I don't very often. I was on the bench over there when I saw you. What exactly are you doing, anyway?"

She laughed. "I suppose it must look a bit strange."

"Yeah, just a bit."

"I'm throwing a ball for Albert."

Albert had been Mad's dog when she was a child. I looked around, but I couldn't see him or the ball.

"Is Albert here now?"

"Yeah, he's there look. Oh, wait! You can't see him, can you?" She put her hand in her pocket and pulled out a pair of the ghostvision glasses which I'd worn once before. "Put these on."

"Won't I look a bit conspicuous?"

"Not really. They look like sunglasses."

Once I was wearing them, sure enough, there was Albert, the German Shepherd, looking every bit as fierce as I remembered. He had a ball in his mouth.

"I didn't think he was able to come to the human world."

"He can only stay for short periods, so every now and then, when it's a nice day, we like to come here during my lunch hour. It breaks the day up. Why don't you throw the ball for him?"

"Okay. Why not?"

I bent down, picked up the ball and threw it as far as I could. Albert chased after it, grabbed it in his teeth, then came rushing back and dropped it between me and Mad.

"Do you like it any better at the library?" I asked, as I threw the ball again.

"Not really. It's so boring. I spend all day stamping books, looking for books, putting books on shelves, and trying not to fall asleep."

"Isn't there another job you could do?"

"That's what I keep asking my bosses in Ghost Town. Surely there has to be something that's more exciting than this. But they won't budge; they insist that the more boring the job, the better the cover. Well, they've certainly achieved that because I'm bored out of my skull."

"We should have a night out sometime," I said.

"What about Kathy? Would she come with us?"

"Don't mention it to her. If she comes, she'll be on my case all night. Let's keep it to me and you; just like the good old days. It'll be a laugh. Anyway, I'd better be making tracks."

"Okay. I'm just going to throw the ball a few more times, and then I'll get back to the excitement which is Washbridge Public Library."

***

That evening, I arrived five minutes early for my date with James Keeper, and recognised him immediately. He was just as handsome in the flesh, but he did have a curious dress sense. His shoes, trousers and jacket were all black, which in itself wasn't too unusual, but his shirt and tie were black as well. Even his hair was jet black.

"Jill?" He had a lovely smile.

"James?"

"Call me Jim, please. I'm so pleased you agreed to meet me. I read your profile, and thought we were a perfect match. Can I get you a drink?"

"I'll just have a soda water, please."

Jim seemed quite interested in what I did for a living, and why I'd decided to use Love Spell. He talked about himself, but didn't tell me anything of any substance. I tried a couple of times to find out what he did for a living, but he seemed to sidestep the question.

About thirty minutes in, there was a commotion at a

table in a corner of the bar, and I heard a woman scream. When I glanced over, I could see a man lying on the floor with people gathered around him.

"Excuse me, Jill," Jim said. "I'd better go and see to this."

"Oh? Okay."

He bent over the prone man. Was he trying to revive him? Perhaps he was a doctor? I quite liked the idea of dating a doctor. A few minutes later, Jim came back.

"How is he?"

"He's passed."

Shortly after, the ambulance arrived. It was rather upsetting to see them put the man in a body bag, and take him away.

"Are you a doctor, Jim?"

"Me, a doctor? No." He appeared to find that quite amusing.

"It didn't say on your profile what you do for a living."

"Look, Jill, I had hoped this might not crop up on our first date, but the truth is, I know you're a witch."

"You do?"

"Yes. I realise this will come as a bit of a surprise, but I'm not a human, either."

"Really? What kind of sup are you then?" I could usually sense what kind of sup someone was, but I couldn't get a read on him at all.

"I'm not a sup either."

"So you're not a human and you're not a sup?"

"That's right."

"What are you, then?"

"I'm a reaper."

"Like a farmer?"

"No, not that kind of reaper. The grim variety."

"A grim reaper?"

"Shh, don't say it too loudly. It tends to scare people."

I wasn't surprised; it scared me. "So what do you do exactly?"

"Pretty much what you'd expect. When someone dies, I come along and help them to the next place."

"Ghost Town, you mean?"

"Some go via Ghost Town."

"Is that what happened just now?"

"Yes. I'm not really supposed to be on duty, but seeing as I was close by, it seemed silly not to process him."

"Process?"

"Sorry, that's the technical jargon. Maybe 'help him', would sound better?"

Then something occurred to me. "Wait a minute. I've just realised—you're Jim Keeper the grim reaper."

"That's not actually my real name."

"I thought not. So what is it?"

"Timothy."

"Tim Keeper the grim reaper?"

"Jim sounds so much better than Tim, don't you think?"

I was lost for words.

"I hope this doesn't change anything?" he said. "The whole grim reaper thing?"

"No, no, of course not." Let me out of here! Now!

"Good. Maybe we could meet up again, then?"

"Yeah, sure. I'll give Love Spell a call." The day after the tenth of never.

Chapter 24

I thought, at first, that it was one of *those* phone calls. You know, the heavy breather type. I was just about to give whoever it was a mouthful, when I realised, it was Amber. She sounded absolutely awful.

"Amber? Are you okay?"

"Jill, can you come over?"

"What's wrong?"

"Pearl and I are both poorly. Could you come over, please? We really could do with some help."

I could hardly say no because she sounded at death's door.

"Okay. I'll be there in a couple of minutes. Are you in the shop?"

"We're upstairs. The shop's closed at the moment. See you soon."

"Was that one of those giddy cousins of yours again?"

"Yes. They're not well."

"Tough! They should just power through."

"That's rich coming from you."

"What do you mean?"

"Every time you have a snuffle, you think you're dying."

"I do not!"

"Of course you do—you're a man."

When I arrived outside Cuppy C, sure enough, it was closed. There was a handwritten note on the inside of the door which read: *Open in thirty minutes*. They must have been confident that I would come over.

I let myself in, and locked the door behind me. Then I

hurried upstairs, and checked the first bedroom where Amber was tucked up in bed.

"Are you awake?"

"Aaghh."

"Amber? Are you okay?"

"Aaghh."

I made my way over to the bed, and saw two eyes peeking out from under the duvet.

"Hi, Jill. Thanks for coming over."

"What's wrong?"

"We've got some kind of twenty-four-hour bug, I think."

"Is Pearl the same?"

"Yeah, we've both got it."

"Why didn't you ask your assistants to run the tea room?"

"It's their day off. I tried to ring them, but they didn't pick up. They must have gone out already. So we thought you could run the tea room today."

"By myself?"

"Yeah. Why not?"

"You two are always telling me that I'm useless behind the counter. How will I cope alone?"

"You'll be all right. It's only for one day. It's usually quiet today, anyway. Will you do it, please? We don't want to leave the shop closed all day."

"I guess so. Is there anything you'd like me to get for you?"

"No, I'm okay, thanks. I just want to go back to sleep."

"I hope you feel better soon. See you later."

Poor Amber.

I made my way along the corridor to the next bedroom.

"Pearl?"

"Hello, Jill."

"Are you okay?"

"No, not really. We've got flu. Did Amber tell you?"

"Yeah."

"Did she ask if you'd look after the shop?"

"Yeah, I will. As long as you trust me to."

"Of course we do."

"Is there anything you'd like me to get for you?"

"A glass of water, please."

I fetched her the water, and put it on the bedside cabinet.

"Anything else?"

"No, that's all, thanks."

"Is Barry at Aunt Lucy's?"

"Yeah, we took him over there yesterday." She rolled over. "I'm going back to sleep now."

"Okay. Don't worry about the shop. I'll see to it."

"Thanks, Jill."

I always felt like the twins were watching me when I was behind the counter—watching and waiting for me to make a mistake. If I was on my own, I wouldn't have to worry about that. This was my opportunity to show the twins what I was made of. The more I thought about it, the more I was warming to the idea.

I went downstairs, and checked in the back for deliveries. The twins had managed to unload them before they went to bed, but they still needed to be put out. To fortify myself for the day ahead, I helped myself to a small blueberry muffin.

What? It was going to be a busy day; I would need the

calories. And besides, it was payment in kind, in advance.

By the time I'd finished putting out all the cakes and pastries, I was ready for a sit down. But then I noticed there were a few people outside the door, waving to me. I'd totally forgotten about the customers. Silly me. I pulled off the temporary 'Closed' notice, unlocked the door and let them in.

"Where are the twins?" A young wizard said.

"Amber and Pearl are poorly today. I'm running the tea room."

"Are you their cousin Jill?"

"Yeah."

"Oh, dear." He laughed.

"What's so funny?"

"The twins told me about you. I was going to have one of their new lattes, but perhaps I ought to stick with something simple."

Cheek of the man! I could make fancy lattes.

Within moments of opening, there was a queue stretching from the counter all the way back to the door. Oh, dear. This was going to be a long day. Still, I could cope.

What could possibly go wrong?

***

What a morning! I'd never stopped. My legs and back were aching, and I had a blinding headache. I'd been desperate for a pee for the best part of an hour, and in the end, I'd had to ask the next person in the queue to wait while I rushed upstairs. I couldn't hear any sound from the twins' bedrooms. They must have been fast asleep. I just hoped they appreciated all the work I was doing. Running Cuppy C all by myself was no joke. At least there was one assistant working in the cake shop or it would have been absolutely impossible.

There had been a queue all morning. I wasn't sure if that was because it was busier than usual or if I was just really, really slow. It wasn't just a matter of trying to serve everyone; I had to clear the tables, and load the dishwasher. I'd run out of cups at one point. It was beyond a joke.

Then, to top it all, there were all the complaints:
"I asked for two shots, not one."
"I asked for skinny, not whole milk."
"I just like to moan – blah, blah and even more blah."

What's the matter with people? I don't know why they need to be so particular over their drinks. What do you mean? Precision with sugar is an entirely different matter.

I was absolutely starving. There I was, handing out delicious muffins to all and sundry, and I hadn't had so much as a crumb to eat since first thing that morning. I wasn't sure I was going to make it through to the end of the day.

By three o'clock, I could see a light at the end of the tunnel. The queue had gone, and there were only a few customers in the shop. I actually managed to grab another muffin, but I had to eat it on the go.

What if the twins were still poorly tomorrow? Would they expect me to do this all over again? I didn't think I could. It would kill me. Maybe some of their assistants would be in by then.

After this, the twins had better not say that I was hopeless behind the counter ever again.

"Hi, Jill."

"Oh? Hi, Hilary." I'd been so preoccupied that I hadn't seen Hilary from Love Spell walk in.

"How did your date go?"

"Don't ask."

"Oh dear. What went wrong?"

"You remember James Keeper's profile didn't show his occupation?"

"Yeah?"

"Well, I discovered what he does." I lowered my voice so no one else could hear. "He's a grim reaper."

"No!"

"Yes! Jim Keeper, the grim reaper. Well, Tim actually."

"You're kidding."

"Does it look like I'm kidding?"

"I'm so sorry, Jill. I don't know how he slipped through. I'll have him removed from our books immediately."

"It's okay. I can laugh about it now, but I didn't think it was funny at the time. Anyway, it looks like you've been shopping."

She was laden with carrier bags from designer boutiques, shoe shops and various department stores.

"Yeah, well it is Premium Day."

"What's that?"

"Haven't you heard of it?"

"I can't say I have."

"It's a really big deal here in Candlefield. Lots of retailers hold huge sales on Premium Day. The date is never announced in advance—nobody knows what day it's going to take place until the night before."

"So it's not on the same day every year?"

"No. That's the whole point. Every year the retailers

pick a date, but they keep it secret, and only announce it around nine o'clock on the previous evening. Then everybody goes wild. You should get down there, Jill. There are some real bargains to be had. The whole town centre is absolutely buzzing."

"Chance would be a fine thing. I'm busy running this place by myself."

"I guessed as much when I saw Pearl and Amber in the shoe shop. I thought—"

"Hang on. Just rewind. When you did what?"

"When I saw Pearl and Amber. They were trying on shoes."

"When was this?"

"A couple of hours ago, I guess."

"You saw Pearl and Amber a couple of hours ago, trying on shoes?"

"Yeah. Didn't they ask you to go with them?"

"No. Funnily enough, they didn't."

I served Hilary with a drink and a muffin, and then marched upstairs. When I pulled back the duvet on Amber's bed, there were two pillows stuffed underneath it. Next door, in Pearl's bedroom, it was the same story.

Those conniving little so-and-so's. They must have found out that it was Premium Day late last night, realised they had no one to run Cuppy C, and come up with a plot to get me to cover for them. If they'd said they wanted to go shopping, I'd have probably refused. By pretending to be poorly, they'd played on my good nature, and conned me into doing it. I couldn't believe it.

Just wait until they got back. I'd make them pay for this.

***

The twins were still not back when it was time to close Cuppy C, so I cashed up, but didn't hang around. If I had, I might have regretted my actions. Instead, I just left them both identical notes, pinned to their pillows: *Revenge will be sweet*.

Before going home, I called in at the office. Unusually, Mrs V wasn't at her desk; she'd left a note to say she had a dental appointment. Winky was fast asleep, and didn't stir.

I was still fuming about the trick the twins had pulled on me. They were going to get theirs—oh yeah!

The room suddenly became a little colder—something that usually happened just before my mother made an appearance.

"Mum?"

There was no sign of her.

Then the chair in front of my desk swivelled a little to the left.

"Mum? Are you there?"

The voice made me jump back in my seat. It wasn't my mother—it was a man's voice, but it was very faint.

"Alberto?"

"Jill?"

The voice was so quiet that I could only just make it out. It didn't sound like Alberto, and yet it was curiously familiar.

"Jill?"

It was a little louder this time. And now I recognised it.

"Colonel?"

"Jill, can you see me?"

"No."

"How about now?"

"Still no."

"I'll never master this stupid 'attaching' business. How about now?"

And there he was—hovering above the chair opposite me. It was definitely the colonel, but a slightly younger version than the one I'd known.

"I can see you. It's so wonderful to have you back."

"It's good to be back. I never used to believe in ghosts, but I'm jolly glad I was wrong. I hope you don't mind me attaching myself to you—I don't really have any family. At least none I want to see again."

"What about Mrs Burnbridge?"

"I think the shock would kill her." He laughed. "You don't seem too fazed, though."

"You aren't my first ghost."

"That's good then. Look, I can't stay long. I find all this exhausting. I just wanted to thank you for helping the police to find out who did this to me."

"I'm sorry it turned out to be Ben."

"Me too, but rather that than have an innocent man like Peter locked up."

"How are you settling in GT?"

"I see you have all the lingo down." He laughed. "Okay, so far. There are an awful lot of pretty lady ghosts. Not that I've noticed, obviously."

"Obviously."

Just then, I heard the outer office door open.

"Sounds like you have a visitor," the colonel said. "I'd better be off. Thanks again, Jill. I'll pop in from time to time if that's okay with you?"

"Of course. Don't be a stranger."

Chapter 25

"Are you talking to yourself again?" Grandma said, as she burst into my office.

"If you must know, I was talking to Colonel Briggs. Or at least his ghost."

"Just be careful you don't allow too many ghosts to attach themselves to you. If you get a reputation for being an easy touch, they'll be queuing up to waste your time. There's nothing more boring than ghost chit chat. Ghost Town this, Ghost Town that, blah, blah, blah."

"The colonel was a good friend. I was pleased to see him again."

"Don't say I didn't warn you."

"Did you want something in particular, Grandma, or is this just a social call?"

"I don't do social calls. My time is much too precious. I came to tell you that I've put your name down for the Compass competition."

"The what?"

"Is there something wrong with your hearing? The Compass competition."

"What's that?"

"It's an annual competition for witches. There are four teams based upon the four quadrants of the compass: The North, which is us, the South, the West, and the East. I've put your name down to be in the North team."

"But I'm only a level three witch. What can I do?"

"The competition is for level three witches and above. You'll be competing against level three witches from the other quadrants. The North has won the competition for the last two years, and we expect to win it again. Needless to say, I am the captain of the North team."

"How many competitions are there? I mean, there's the Levels competition and the Elite competition, and now there's—what's it called again?"

Grandma sighed. "The Compass competition. It isn't difficult to remember. That's why the teams are North, South, West, and East."

"Are there any other competitions?"

"The three you just mentioned are the main ones. There are others, but they're for the other sups."

"Is there a competition which includes all the sups?"

"There used to be one. It ran for many years, but hasn't been held for twenty years or more."

"Why's that?"

"You ask a lot of questions. There's a natural rivalry between different kinds of sups. For the most part, it's kept under control in day-to-day life, but during the competitions, the worst elements can bubble to the surface. It became too dangerous."

"What was that competition called?"

"The Valour." Grandma was growing impatient. "Enough of the history lesson. That competition is dead and buried. I doubt we'll see the likes of it again. You need to focus on the Compass. I expect you to put in a lot of practise over the coming days to make sure you're ready for it."

"When is it?"

"A week on Saturday."

"Why didn't you tell me earlier?"

"I shouldn't have to. You should make it your business to keep abreast of Candlefield news and events."

"I check the notice board in Cuppy C regularly."

"Oh, well, that's okay then." Grandma shook her head in obvious exasperation. "Because that is obviously the centre of the universe in terms of news and current affairs. What about reading The Candle, for a start?"

"I don't read many newspapers. I generally check the news online."

"There is no *online* in Candlefield. You'd better start to read the papers, talk to people, and find out what's happening. If you ever want to be a level six witch, then you need to act like a witch, not like a human who is only there on vacation."

"Okay, sorry. I'll start to read The Candle. What sort of spells should I practise?"

"Oh dearie, dearie me. How many times do I have to tell you? Once you get to level three, it's not about practising individual spells. It's about spell selection, and adapting spells to meet your particular need. Have you already forgotten what happened when we went underground in the Range?"

"Of course not. Look, I'm wearing the pendant."

"You got that because you made it through the obstacle course, and you did that because you selected the correct spells. That's precisely what the Compass competition will require of you. Don't waste your time practising individual spells. You already know them off by heart, or at least you should. Think more about how to focus on those spells, and how to adapt them for the situation. The Compass competition is not going to be easy. Don't think you can just turn up and expect to win. You'll need to put in hours of practise beforehand."

"How many others will be on our team?"

"There are four members in each team."

"Just four?"

"One for each of the levels. You will be our representative at level three."

"But that's crazy. I've only just moved up to that level. There must be lots of more experienced level three witches in the North quadrant."

"Are you questioning your captain's team selection?"

"No, but—"

"Good. Just make sure you don't let me down."

With that, she disappeared.

Oh bum!

***

After yet another crazy day, I was glad to be going home. I just wanted to get back to the flat, and have a quiet night in by myself. Just me, a good book and a few custard creams. I had to make sure I didn't bump into Mr Ivers or Betty Longbottom; I couldn't cope with either of them today.

"Jill!"

The voice caught me by surprise. It wasn't Mr Ivers and it wasn't Betty Longbottom, but it *was* somebody who I would quite gladly have never seen again: Dougal Andrews from The Bugle, or as I preferred to think of him, Dougal Bugle.

"What do you want, Dougal?"

"Nice to see you, too, Jill. It's been a while. I thought you might be missing me."

"Yeah. Like the plague."

"That's not very nice."

"Did you want something?"

"Just a few moments of your time, if that's possible."

"It's not possible. Not now, not ever. I've told you before, I won't be doing any more interviews for your rag after the way you misrepresented what I said last time."

"Are you still harping on about that? Time to let it go. That's history, now. No one even cares."

"I care. You promised the article wouldn't be a hatchet job on the police, and that I'd be able to see it before it was published. It was, and you didn't. We're done." I tried to push past him, but he blocked my way.

"If you don't get out of my way, Dougal, I won't be responsible for my actions."

"You're not threatening me, are you?"

"I'm not threatening; I'm promising."

"Look, the reason I'm here is that we're going to be running an article in the morning, and out of courtesy, I thought I should give you the chance to comment before it's published."

I didn't like the sound of this, not one bit. "What article is that?"

"I think you'll like the headline: *Slavery is alive and well in Washbridge.*"

Slavery? What did I know about modern day slavery, and why would he want my comments? "I don't know what you're talking about, Dougal. Get out of the way. I've had a hard day."

"That's disappointing because you are actually the focus of the article."

"What do I have to do with slavery?"

"According to my sources, your P.A, Mrs Annabel Versailles, is forced to work for you without any pay. I'd call that slavery. What would you call it?"

I could feel my blood pressure rising. I wanted to kill the man. To tear his head off and kick it around the floor.

"That's rubbish. Where did you get your information from?"

"You should know by now that a newspaper reporter never reveals his sources. So, would you care to comment?"

"Yeah, here's a comment for you. You're ugly, overweight and have bad breath. And you can quote me on that."

***

Back in my flat, my head was still buzzing with thoughts of the Compass competition. I was nervous, but excited too. I'd done well in the Levels, but that was an individual competition where the only person I could let down was myself. The Compass competition was a whole different ball game. This was a team event, so if I messed up, I would be letting the whole team down. And that wouldn't go down well with the team captain.

No pressure then.

As I studied my reflection in the mirror, I took hold of the pendant which I wore around my neck every day with a sense of pride. Suddenly, the strangest sensation passed through my body—an icy shiver which chilled me to the bone.

That's when I heard the voice.

"You will take it to a new level."

ALSO BY ADELE ABBOTT

The Witch P.I. Mysteries:

Witch Is When... (Books #1 to #12)
Witch Is When It All Began
Witch Is When Life Got Complicated
Witch Is When Everything Went Crazy
Witch Is When Things Fell Apart
Witch Is When The Bubble Burst
Witch Is When The Penny Dropped
Witch Is When The Floodgates Opened
Witch Is When The Hammer Fell
Witch Is When My Heart Broke
Witch Is When I Said Goodbye
Witch Is When Stuff Got Serious
Witch Is When All Was Revealed

Witch Is Why... (Books #13 to #24)
Witch Is Why Time Stood Still
Witch is Why The Laughter Stopped
Witch is Why Another Door Opened
Witch is Why Two Became One
Witch is Why The Moon Disappeared
Witch is Why The Wolf Howled
Witch is Why The Music Stopped
Witch is Why A Pin Dropped
Witch is Why The Owl Returned
Witch is Why The Search Began
Witch is Why Promises Were Broken
Witch is Why It Was Over

The Susan Hall Mysteries:
Whoops! Our New Flatmate Is A Human.
Whoops! All The Money Went Missing.
Whoops! There's A Canary In My Coffee
See web site for availability.

AUTHOR'S WEB SITE
http:www.AdeleAbbott.com

FACEBOOK
http://www.facebook.com/AdeleAbbottAuthor

MAILING LIST
(new release notifications only)
http:/AdeleAbbott.com/adele/new-releases/

Printed in Great Britain
by Amazon